The Magic Unicorn

Bedtime Stories for Kids
Short Funny, Fantasy Stories for Children
and Toddlers to Help Them Fall Asleep
and Relax. Fantastic Stories to Dream
about for All Ages. Easy to Read.

D1316456

Table of Contents

Introduction

Congratulations on purchasing *The Magic Unicorn* and thank you for doing so.

The following chapters are easy to read bedtime stories to help your child or toddler to fall asleep and dream happy dreams.

There are plenty of books on this subject on the market, thanks again for choosing this one! The goal of the author is to keep the stories light, funny, and entertaining, while at the same time cover topics that your child can learn and grow into. Sweet Dreams!

Animal Friends

The Unicorn and the Frog

There once was a magic unicorn named Brindle. She was a beautiful white unicorn with a special gold horn that sparkled in the light. Brindle was a very special little unicorn, just like all other unicorns are special. One thing that made Brindle extra special was that she was a magical unicorn!

Brindle loved to do the things that all other little unicorns did... jump and play in the sunlight... dance and sing in the rain... But more than anything else, Brindle was a curious little unicorn who liked to ask lots of questions; and more than anything else, Brindle loved making new friends.

So it was, one cool, rainy day, Brindle was out and about, singing and dancing in the rain like she loved to do, when she heard an unusual sound.

Bru-u-u-p.

Brindle stopped her little dance and went very quiet. She waited, and then she heard it again, with a new sound thrown in.

Bru-u-u-p. Bro-o-o-p.

It was a weird, vibrating sound, but Brindle found it very interesting. Being the very curious little unicorn that she was, Brindle went in search to see where the sound was coming from.

Bru-u-u-p. Bro-o-o-p. Bra-a-a-p.

Brindle was becoming more and more curious. She looked behind a tree. It wasn't coming from there. She looked behind a rock. It wasn't coming from there.

Bru-u-u-p. Bro-o-o-p. Bra-a-a-p.

So, where was it coming from? Brindle saw some water in the distance and decided that maybe it was coming from there, so there she went.

Bru-u-u-p. Bro-o-o-p. Bra-a-a-p.

When she reached the edge of the water, she saw a little green creature with big yellow eyes, sitting on a rock at the edge of the water.

Bru-u-u-p. Bro-o-o-p. Bra-a-a-p.

"It's you!" Brindle smiled happily.

The little creature was startled and looked at Brindle with its big blinking yellow eyes.

Bru-u-u-p. "I mean... who me? What is me?" The little frog said, the sound coming out first.

"Why, it's you making that beautiful sound!" Brindle's smile got even bigger. "What kind of creature are you?"

"Me?" The little creature asked in surprise. "I'm a frog!"

Then it hung its little head in sadness.

"What is wrong?" Brindle asked, feeling the little frog's sadness. One of Brindle's magic powers was that she could feel what others felt through her magic horn. "Don't be sad! What is your name?"

"My name is Brup." The little frog said. "And I'm sad because my brother and sister, Brop and Brap, are off running around somewhere and we always sing together in the rain. Now I am here, trying to sing all by myself."

"It can feel sad when you have no one else to sing with," Brindle nodded in agreement. "But singing is about being happy. I was just out singing in the rain by myself. It's okay to do the things you love when you're alone too."

"I know," Brup sighed. "But it's much more fun to do them with someone else."

"It is," Brindle agreed. "And then she got an idea. "Why don't I sing with you until your brother and sister come home? I love to sing in the rain too!"

"Will you do that?" The frog asked hopefully.

"Of course! Brindle said. "What do you want to sing?"

"Let's sing the name song!" Brup said excitedly. "It was the song I was trying to sing when you showed up.

"The name song sounds perfect!" Brindle did a little unicorn dance. "My name is Brindle."

"Okay... I'll start," the little frog said happily. "Bru-u-u-p!" The little frog turned its name into a sing-song pretty little vibrating sound.

"Bri-i-i-ndle!" The little unicorn sang out, her horn tinkling with little musical notes.

"How wonderful!" Brup said and continued.

Bru-u-u-p.

Bri-i-i-ndle.

Bru-u-u-p.

Bri-i-i-ndle.

The two new friends kept singing the name song together until the rain stopped and the sun came out.

"That was so much fun!" Brup said at the end. "Thank you for singing with me. You have a beautiful name, song sound."

"Thank you!" Brindle said happily. "I love your name song sound too. Maybe we can sing together in the rain again sometime."

"I would really love that," Brup said with a smile. "It helps to make a rainy day more special."

"All days are special!" Brindle laughed. "Thank you for sharing your song with me. Now I have something new that I can do when I'm alone on a rainy day, and I will always think of you."

"Thanks again, Brindle," the frog gave a little hop. "I see my brother and sister coming back now. Thank you for making my day not so lonely. Now, if I'm ever feeling alone on a rainy day again, I can sing the name song and think of you and not feel alone anymore."

"Have a great rest of your day!" Brindle said as she turned and danced away into the sun.

The Unicorn and the Caterpillar

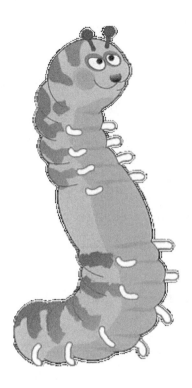

Brindle the magic unicorn was a beautiful white unicorn with a special gold horn that sparkled in the light. More than anything else in the whole world, Brindle loved helping people, learning new things, and making new friends!

One day, when Brindle was walking along in the sunshine, she heard a little voice crying. Because she was a magic unicorn, she could also feel how sad and afraid the person was. Brindle looked around until she spotted a tiny fuzzy creature with a bunch of legs sitting on the leaf of a nearby plant.

It made Brindle feel unhappy whenever someone else was sad, so she went over to see whether there was anything that she could do to help.

"What is the matter, little friend?" Brindle asked the fuzzy little creature. The little creature looked up at Brindle, stopping what he was doing.

"I am afraid," the little creature replied. "My mommy told me that everything is about to change, and I am afraid of change. I like things the way they are. New things scare me."

"Well, what kind of change is going to happen?" Brindle asked.

"I d-d-don't know!" The little creature sobbed. "I didn't understand what my mommy was trying to tell me. It all sounded so scary!"

"Ahhh, I see." Brindle nodded in understanding. "You are afraid of the unknown."

"The unknown... is that some kind of monster?" The little creature shivered.

"No," Brindle giggled. "The unknown is just things we don't know. When we don't know things or understand things, it makes them feel very scary. But really, the unknown is just a big, new adventure!"

"Really?" The little creature asked, hopefully.

"Really." Brindle nodded. "What is your name?"

"I am Cal," the little creature answered. "And I am a caterpillar."

"A caterpillar! How wonderful!" Brindle smiled. "My name is Brindle, and I'm a unicorn."

"I have never seen a unicorn before," Cal said with a smile. Then he gave a big yawn.

"Are you sleepy?" Brindle asked with concern.

"Yes," Cal said. "When I started getting really sleepy, that's when my mommy said that I had a change coming in my life. She showed me how to make this blanket I have been working on to keep me safe."

"Well, I can help keep you safe, if you'd like," Brindle offered. "I can stand and watch over you while you sleep."

"That would be wonderful!" Cal said excitedly. He started working on his blanket even faster to get it done.

"How fun!" Brindle said, watching him work. "You are building the blanket around you, and wrapping it all around yourself!"

"My mommy told me that it was called a cocoon," Cal said, close to finishing his work.

"Okay," Brindle said with a smile. "You finish that last little bit to get your head covered and go to sleep. I will protect you and be here when you wake up."

"Thank you, Brindle," Cal said, his eyes getting very sleepy. "You are a very good friend. I am glad we met."

Cal finished his cocoon and wrapped the last bits of himself uptight. Brindle gave him a gentle little touch of her horn, and a magic glow surrounded Cal's cocoon to protect him.

Brindle waited and waited while several days passed, and Cal was still asleep. She never left her friend's side the whole time. Then one day, the little cocoon surrounding Cal started to move.

Brindle was excited to watch as Cal's cocoon split open and he started struggling to come out. When he was finished, Brindle jumped and danced and laughed.

"Cal, change really did happen to you!" Brindle said happily.

The Unicorn and the Fake Unicorn

Brindle the magic unicorn was a beautiful white unicorn with a special gold horn that sparkled in the light. More than anything else in the whole world, Brindle loved helping people, learning new things, and making new friends!

It was a bright sunny day and Brindle was out happily playing in the sunshine when she came across another unicorn.

"How exciting!" Brindle said when she came face to face with the other unicorn. "It is a special day when I get to meet another unicorn."

The other unicorn didn't say anything at first, she just looked at Brindle with worry on her face.

"What's wrong?" Brindle asked. "You seem very worried."

"I'm not," the other unicorn sniffed and turned her head away. "I am just a very busy little unicorn and don't have time to play."

"But that's what unicorns do!" Brindle said in surprise. "We were born to play by the magic that created us!"

"Well, er, of course, we were!" The other unicorn said. "I just have more important things to do right now."

"What is your name?" Brindle asked, trying to come around so that she was face to face with the other unicorn again, but the other unicorn kept turning away. "My name is Brindle."

"I am Mari," the other unicorn replied. "Now go away. I don't have time to play."

"Okay," Brindle said, a little hurt and confused. But she could still feel that Mari was nervous. "Mari..."

The other unicorn turned around quickly at the sound of her name, and her horn slipped down over her eye. Brindle looked closer and saw that it was a wooden horn tied onto her head with ribbon.

"Why, you're not a unicorn! You're a horse!" Brindle said in surprise.

Mari started crying. "These children started teasing me and saying how ugly I was. I just wanted to be beautiful. And the most beautiful thing I know of is a unicorn. I just wanted the others to stop saying mean things about me."

"Oh!" Brindle said in surprise. "Well, thank you! But I think you're beautiful just the way you are. You don't have to pretend to be something you're not."

"Really?" Mari sniffed, her tears stopping. "You think I'm beautiful?"

"Yes!" Brindle said with enthusiasm. "Let me show you!"

"Okay," Mari said, a little nervous.

"It will be fine," Brindle reassured her.

Brindle use her horn to untie the fake horn from around Mari's neck, and then let the gold magic come from out of her horn to brush out Mari's mane and tail. She then used the ribbon from the horn to tie pretty little bows on Mari's mane. They went down to the river so that Brindle could help Mari wash her tears away.

Brindle stepped back. "Look at how beautiful you are!"

Mari looked at her reflection in the river water and gasped. "I *am* beautiful!"

"Yes, you are!" Brindle laughed happily. "You are beautiful just the way you are. Don't ever let anyone make you feel that you should be something other than who and what you are. We are all unique and special."

"Thank you, Brindle," Mari said. "Thank you for showing me that I just need to be myself."

"Any time, Mari!" Brindle said with a smile. "Even if you are not a unicorn, I think it's time to play!"

"Okay!" Mari said as they happily chased each other into the sunlight.

The Unicorn and the Fish

Brindle the magic unicorn was a beautiful white unicorn with a special gold horn that sparkled in the light. More than anything else in the whole world, Brindle loved helping people, learning new things, and making new friends!

One day, Brindle was walking down the beach, feeling the warmth of the sunshine on her little unicorn face. Suddenly, she heard a *splash* in the water. She looked but didn't see anything.

Then she heard it again. *Splash*. Brindle tried looking closer, still not seeing anything. Suddenly, the splash came again, but this time, it was right at her nose in the water and got her whole face wet.

Brindle laughed, shaking the drops of water from her face. A scaly wet face appeared from out of the water.

"A fish!" Brindle said happily. "What is your name?"

"I don't have a name," said the little fish. "I am just a fish, like all of the others."

"You are not just like everyone else," Brindle said with a smile. "We are all different. Maybe we should give you a name!"

"What name should I have?" The little fish looked hopeful.

"I don't know," Brindle said. "Let's try a few and see what one suits you the best."

"Hmmm... let's see...." Brindle eyed the little fish. "You don't look like a George... or a Harry... or a Timmy..."

"No," the little fish agreed. "None of those sound like me."

"Maybe we can use my magic horn to find out what your name should be," Brindle said.

"How do we do that?" The little fish asked.

"Like this," Brindle replied. "I think about what your name should be, and then point my horn at you..."

Golden magic glitter glowed from Brindle's horn and settled on the little fish.

"Freeman!" The little fish said suddenly. "My name is Freeman!"

"Do you like your new name?" Brindle asked.

"I do!" Freeman said. "I like it very much. Wait... you never told me your name."

"I am Brindle," said the little magic unicorn. "And I have a new friend named Freeman."

"Would you like to play with me, Brindle?" Freeman asked.

"I would!" Brindle laughed.

Freeman and Brindle spent the rest of the sunny day splashing each other and playing in the water, each having fun with their newfound friend.

The Unicorn and the Beaver

Brindle was a very special unicorn. She was bright white with a beautiful glowing gold horn. Brindle loved to make new friends and help people. Best of all, Brindle was a magical unicorn!

On this bright and sunny day, Brindle's golden horn sparkled under the sunlight. She was walking along the water, looking for her friend, Freeman, to see if he wanted to play today. But Freeman was nowhere to be found. Brindle wasn't unhappy about it, though; she was glad that Freeman was off having his own adventures.

While she was walking along the edge of the water looking for her fishy friend, she came across a furry little creature with a wide flat tail, running back and forth between the water and the trees.

"Oh my!" said Brindle. "That is quite the thing you are building!"

"I don't have time to chat," the furry little creature said, continuing to run back and forth. He would run into the trees and coming running back out with branches and other bits of wood. Those bits would be stacked on top of the other ones already in the water, and he would start all over again.

"Are you building a bridge?" Brindle asked.

"No," said the creature, "I am building a dam to slow the river down right here so that it doesn't wash my home away." And off he went again.

"A dam?" Brindle asked. She thought about it for a second. Then she realized... "Oh! You must be a beaver!"

"Benni Beaver," the creature replied as he brought out another pile of wood.

"Can I help?" Brindle asked.

"I don't know how," Benni said, continuing to work. But he pointed to his house in the water behind the dam, a large mound of sticks and wood sticking up out of the center of the river. "I have to hurry before my house floats away!"

Brindle looked at Benni's house and saw that it was breaking apart slowly, one little stick at a time floating down the river. She frowned, thinking hard. Then she had an idea.

"I can help," said Brindle. "My name is Brindle, and I'm a magical unicorn! I don't know how to build dams, but I can help you protect your home while you build your dam."

"Really?" Benni asked, hopefully.

"Of course!" Brindle announced. She walked closer to the water's edge and stuck her horn into the water. A golden glow spread out and moved to cover Benni's house and keep all of the pieces from floating away in the fast river waters.

"Oh! Oh! Oh!" Benni the beaver jumped up and down in excitement. "You really *are* magic! Thank you, Brindle!"

"Of course!" Brindle said, happy to be able to help.

She relaxed by the water, using her magic horn to hold Benni's house together while he finished building the dam. Then he came and sat down next to her at the edge of the water.

"Thank you, Brindle. You helped me to save my house," Benni said happily.

"I am happy that I could help, and make a new friend!" Brindle said. She took her horn out of the water and looked at Benni's work. "That is quite a beautiful dam!"

"I built it tall enough just to slow the waters down behind it so that my house stays safe," Benni said.

"Well, your house is safe, and you should be very proud," Brindle replied.

"I *am* proud... I am proud that I have a new friend!" Benni announced.

"Thank you, Benni!" Brindle said with a smile. She and her new friend spent the rest of the lazy afternoon by the river talking about their adventures.

The Unicorn and the Eagle

Brindle was a very special unicorn. She was bright white with a beautiful glowing golden yellow horn. Brindle loved to make new friends and help people. Best of all, Brindle was a magical unicorn!

It was a bright sunny day, and Brindle was walking around, admiring the clouds as they floated across the sky, making shadows on the fields as she walked. It was a happy day!

One shadow moved faster than the others, and Brindle looked up to see a large, beautiful bird flying overhead, circling the spot where she stood in the field. When the bird saw her looking up, it made slow, sweeping circles downward, until it finally landed in the field in front of Brindle.

"Hello there!" The bird smiled at Brindle. "I am Elli the eagle. What is your name? And what kind of creature are you? I have never seen one of you before."

Brindle laughed. "Hi Elli, I am Brindle, and I'm a unicorn. A *magic* unicorn." She added.

"I have never seen a unicorn before!" Elli said excitedly. "I wonder why that is?"

"I don't know, "Brindle said. "Although there aren't that many of us unicorns around. I think that may have something to do with it."

"Maybe," Elli said. "Hey, Brindle... would you like to come flying with me? Unicorns can fly, right? But I thought they were supposed to have wings."

"You are thinking of a Pegasus," Brindle said. "A Pegasus has wings. Unicorns have horns."

"Oh," Elli said. "I was hoping for someone to play within the skies today. I guess I'll just have to keep looking."

Brindle could feel Elli's disappointment.

"Well..." said Brindle, trying to make Elli feel better. "I don't have wings, but I am magic. Maybe I can magic myself into being able to fly with you."

"Really?" Elli asked. "Can you really do that?"

"I don't know," Brindle admitted. "I have never tried. Let me see if I can."

Brindle focused hard on the magic in her horn. She tried to magic herself into flying. But it didn't work. She was disappointed. Worse yet, she could feel that Elli was again disappointed too.

"Oh, well," Elli said. "At least you tried."

"Well..." Brindle thought hard. "Maybe I can't fly that way. But maybe you can pick me up and carry me, and we can fly together!"

Elli looked at Brindle, judging her size. "I am a big bird, for sure. But I don't think that even I could carry a unicorn. You are just too big and heavy."

"My magic may not be able to help me fly," Brindle smiled. "But it can make me smaller!" And with just a thought, Brindle used the magic in her horn, and she started shrinking down to the size of a cat.

"Oh!" Elli said happily. "Now I can carry you!"

"We only have a little bit of time before it wears off," Brindle said. "So, we'd best get this adventure started!"

Elli happily jumped up into the air and then swooped down and picked Brindle up. Together they soared across the sunny sky. Brindle was excited to fly, and she and her new friend chatted happily until it was time to come down again.

The Unicorn and the Lion

Brindle was a very special unicorn. She was bright white with a beautiful glowing gold horn. Brindle loved to make new friends and help people. Best of all, Brindle was a magical unicorn!

Brindle was out walking one day under the trees when she heard someone crying. She could feel the pain that they were in and it made her sad. She wanted to help make their pain go away!

So, Brindle went looking for the source of the crying to see what she could do to help. She came across a yellow cat that was very big and had a large mass of fur circled around its face.

"Oh!" said Brindle. "You are a lion!"

"I am," the lion sad with a tear rolling down its face. "Now go away, before I eat you."

"You're not going to eat me," Brindle said. "I am here to help you."

"How do you think you can help me?" the lion asked. "I have a thorn stuck in my foot, and I can't get it out because I have no hands. I can't use my teeth to get it out because it is too small and stuck in too deep."

"My name is Brindle, and I am a magic unicorn. Surely there is something I can do to help. We can figure out a way."

"You have no hands either," the lion pouted. "My name is Leon, but I still don't see how you are going to be able to help me."

"It's nice to meet you, Leon," Brindle said patiently. "But did you miss the part where I said that I am a magical unicorn?"

"No," said Leon. "I just still don't see how that's going to help."

"Do you mind if I get a little closer?" Brindle asked.

"Okay," Leon replied.

"And you won't try to eat me?"

Leon sighed. "I promise not to try and eat you. But if you can't help me, I'm not going to make any promises about what I might try afterward."

"That's not a very encouraging answer," Brindle said. "But I am still going to try and help you."

Brindle walked over to the lion, keeping an eye out for sudden movements. Leon turned his paw over and showed her where there was a little thorn stuck in between his toes.

"Oh, my," Brindle nodded. "You are right. That is certainly stuck in there deep."

Leon just growled.

"But that doesn't mean I can't help!" Brindle announced. "Hold still."

She lowered her horn down until it touched the thorn. Leon jerked his paw back, and Brindle just looked at him, shaking her head. "I can't do anything if you don't hold still."

Leon looked skeptical but held his paw back out again for Brindle to work her magic. And work her magic she did! Brindle touched her horn again to the thorn and magic sparkles came out to touch the thorn.

Brindle started backing up, and the magic held the thorn onto her horn. She worked very slowly so that she wouldn't cause Leon any more pain. One more step and... there it was! Brindle had pulled the thorn out of Leon's paw!

Leon looked up at Brindle with a smile. "Thank you, Brindle. I'm glad I didn't eat you."

Brindle laughed. "I'm glad you didn't eat me too! But I knew that you wouldn't."

"How did you know?" Leon asked.

"Because even though I was a little nervous, I know that friends don't eat friends," Brindle smiled.

"Then I guess since we are friends now, I will never have to think about eating you again!"

"I am always happy to make new friends," said Brindle.

The Unicorn and the Bear

Brindle was a very special unicorn. She was bright white with a beautiful glowing gold horn. Brindle loved to make new friends and help people. Best of all, Brindle was a magical unicorn!

Today was another day where Brindle found herself walking through the trees. It was shady and cool under the canopy of leaves. She thought about her new friend, Leon, and wondered how he was doing.

On this day, she felt someone else in the woods. It wasn't sadness this time that she felt. Today she felt someone very annoyed and yet still in pain. She didn't understand it, so she decided to go investigate.

Eventually, she came across a large furry animal standing on its hind legs, batting at a beehive. She watched her for a while. The creature would stand up, bat at the beehive, which was just out of her reach. The bees would come out and swarm and sting her. She would have to sit back down, and Brindle could feel that she was both annoyed and in pain. When the bees settled down, the creature would try again.

Finally, Brindle came closer to find out what was going on.

"Hello," Brindle called out as she got closer. "My name is Brindle. I can see that you're having trouble, but I don't understand what you are trying to do."

The creature looked over at Brindle with annoyance. "I'm Berri, and I am trying to get at the honey in that beehive. Now go away and let me get my treat."

Brindle watched again while Berri stood up and swatted at the beehive. After the bees swarmed her and she sat back down, Brindle suddenly realized what was going on.

"Oh! I see..." Brindle said. "You are a bear! I have heard that bears love honey more than anything else."

"Yes, I am a bear," Berri replied, still annoyed. "And what are you?"

"I am a magic unicorn," Brindle answered. "Do you think that maybe the bees are mad at you because you are hurting their home?"

"Of course!" Berri said. "But how else am I supposed to get the honey?"

"Have you tried asking them nicely?" Brindle asked.

"I did try that," Berri sighed. "But they can only bring me tiny little tastes, and that doesn't work."

"But they are okay with giving you honey?" Brindle asked.

"Yes!" Berri said. "But it's not enough."

"It sounds to me like you are being bratty because you are being a little greedy," Brindle said, but not to be mean.

"I know," Berri hung her head, and Brindle could feel that she was a little ashamed. "But I don't know how else to do it."

"Well..." Brindle said. "I am a magic unicorn. I can maybe help you, but first, you need to apologize to the bees for being so greedy and trying to hurt them just to get what you want."

Berri looked up. "I really *am* sorry, you know. I know they were trying to help."

"Don't tell *me*," Brindle said gently. "Tell it to *them*."

Berri looked up at the bees surrounding the beehive and apologized. "I am sorry. I know you were trying to help, and I wasn't being nice about it."

When Brindle could feel that the bees accepted Berri's apology, she nodded. "Okay," she said. "Now, let's try to do this in a way that doesn't hurt anyone."

Berri stepped back from the tree, and Brindle pointed her magic horn up at the beehive. Golden sparkles came from her horn and went into the beehive. When the sparkles came out again, they were dripping with sweet, golden honey.

"Oh!" Berri said happily as the honey floated down to her. Berri held her paws up, and the sparkles covered them in sticky honey.

Berri started licking happily at her paws. "Thank you, Brindle! Now I feel happy!"

"I like to help new friends," Brindle said. "You can come to find me when you feel the need to have honey again, and I will try to help. Just remember that there may always be a better way to get what you want that doesn't hurt other people."

"I will remember that, Brindle," Berri said solemnly. "Thank you for helping me. And I will always try to find a better way."

"Then, this is a happy day!" Brindle laughed and came to share some of the honey with her new friend, Berri.

More Friends

The Unicorn and the Rock

Brindle was a happy, curious, white magical unicorn with a golden horn. More than anything else, she loved helping others and making new friends. Learning new things was always a bonus!

One day, Brindle was walking along between a field of flowers and a forest of trees. The path she was wandering took her directly to a very large rock.

"Hmmm…" Brindle said out loud to herself. "This rock is not in a good place for me. It is very large and difficult to go around."

She heard a long, drawn-out sigh. Looking around, Brindle tried to see where the sigh came from, but couldn't see anyone in sight.

"Who is it?" Brindle called out. "I hear you, but I cannot see you."

The sigh came again, deeper and longer this time. Brindle suddenly realized that it came from the rock in front of her. She looked around but didn't see anyone sitting on the rock, or even behind it.

"This is most puzzling," said Brindle.

"I am sorry that you feel it hard to go around me," a voice suddenly came from the rock. "But you have to understand, you can move and go around. I cannot move at all."

Brindle suddenly felt ashamed. "I am so sorry! I did not mean to make you feel like a burden."

"It's all right," the rock replied. "I am used to it. I watch everyone else move around and see wonderful things that I will never get to see for myself."

"That is so sad!" Brindle said. "Maybe I can help you."

"There is nothing you can do," the rock said patiently. "I am too big to be moved around by anyone, let alone a little unicorn like you."

"But I am a magical unicorn!" Brindle said proudly. "And you are right. Even with my magic, you are too big for me to move around. Even magic has its limits."

The rock sighed again. "I know. It's okay."

Brindle shook her head. "No, it's not okay. I made you feel as though you were in the way when really, there is nothing you can do about it. You are stuck in this place. But what I can do, if it is okay with you, I can use my magic to help you see out and beyond where you are so that you can experience more of the rest of the world."

"You can do that?" The rock asked hopefully.

"I can!" Brindle did a little happy dance. "If it's okay with you...?"

"Oh, yes! Of course! I would love to see the rest of the world!"

Brindle came closer to the rock and touched her magic horn on the stony surface. Sparkling glittering came out of her horn and covered the rock.

"Each piece of glitter will show you a different picture or scene when you look at it," Brindle told the rock with a smile.

"I can see that!" the rock said excitedly. "I never realized how big and beautiful the world really was!"

Brindle laughed at the happiness in the rock's voice.

"I also never knew that there could be such wonderful, helpful creatures in the world," the rock said kindly. "Like you, Brindle. Thank you for such an amazing gift."

"You are most welcome!" Brindle blushed, not used to compliments. "I am glad that I could help you find a way to see the world."

She settled in, leaning against the rock. "Now, tell me what you see."

The rock took his time and shared with Brindle the magic of the sights he was seeing. For Brindle, it was fun, seeing the whole world fresh through someone else's eyes. They continued to share their joy and stories throughout the rest of the afternoon.

The Unicorn and the Field of Flowers

Brindle was a happy, curious, white magical unicorn with a golden horn. More than anything else, she loved helping others and making new friends. Learning new things was just a bonus!

Brindle left her new friend, the rock, after spending the whole night talking about all the new and wonderful things that the rock finally got to experience seeing, thanks to the help of Brindle's magic. Since it was a bright and beautiful sunny day, she went out into the field of flowers instead of continuing her way on the journey she had been taking the day before she met the rock.

The sight of the beautiful field full of flowers made Brindle's heart smile, and she danced around in the sunlight, chasing after all of the colors of the flowers, moving from one to the next. There were red, blue, yellow, orange, and purple flowers all settled into a field of green.

"How wonderful the world of colors is!" Brindle said with a happy smile. "I would love to learn more about colors someday."

"What about learning about the flowers themselves?" a tiny little voice buzzed by her head.

"What do you mean?" Brindle asked. "Who are you?"

"I am Bizzy Bee," the little flying insect moved into Brindle's view. "I and my family help to make more flowers, and help to create all of the beauty that you see in front of you."

"And they say that I am magic," Brindle laughed. "That is a magic trick indeed, making all of the flowers!"

"We don't actually make the flowers," Bizzy said. "But when the time is right, flowers make a little bit of nectar that we go to get in order to fill our beehives with honey."

"Oh!" Brindle said. "Are you one of the bees from where Berri bear was trying to get at the honey?"

"Yes!" Bizzy smiled. "And you helped us so that our home did not get destroyed. We do not like going out and hurting Berri to make her stop, but we did need to protect our home. Thank you, Brindle, for your help back then."

"Just come find me if you need some help again," Brindle offered.

"Thank you!" Bizzy said. "As I was saying, when we go to get the nectar from the flowers to make honey, we brush up against the pollen that the flowers create. When we walk around, we move the pollen into the right place for the flower to make even more flowers."

"That still sounds like magic to me!" Brindle giggled.

"All of nature is magical when you look at it like that," Bizzy said.

"Of course, it is!" Brindle replied. "Don't you think so? I like finding the magic in every part of the world. Learning new things is even magical to me. And you have just taught me something magical about nature, so now I have double magic today!"

"You have triple magic," Bizzy pointed out. "A magical unicorn magically learning a magical thing about nature."

"I do have triple magic today!" Brindle laughed. "Thank you, Bizzy, for sharing such a magical day with me!"

"Any time, Brindle!" Bizzy said as he flew away. "Come by and share a sweet honey treat later on!"

"Thank you, Bizzy," Brindle called back. "I will be there later!"

The Unicorn and the Child

Brindle was a beautiful, white *magical* unicorn. Her favorite things in the whole world were to learn new things, help others, and to make new friends.

One day, Brindle was wandering down by the beach, and she saw a little creature playing in the sand. Only this creature had no fur, except for on top of her little head where she had long, beautiful copper-colored hair. Brindle was very curious. Not too far away from the little creature was another creature, only bigger, laying down to soak up the warmth of the sun.

Brindle wandered over to the little creature. "Hi, there! My name is Brindle. Who are you?"

The little creature looked up at Brindle. "My name is Hannah. What *are* you?"

"I am a unicorn," Brindle replied. "What are you?"

"I am a little girl," said Hannah.

The bigger creature looked up when she heard Hannah talking. "Hannah, honey, who are you talking to?"

"I'm talking to Brindle, Mommy," Hannah answered. "She is a unicorn."

The Mommy creature looked around and then nodded. She laid back down to close her eyes. "Have fun with your imaginary friend, sweetheart. Play nice."

"You're not imaginary, are you?" Hannah asked Brindle.

"No, I'm very real, but I'm also magical," Brindle told Hannah. "Sometimes, when people get older, they forget how to see magical things all around them. I don't think your Mommy sees me."

Hannah thought about this for a minute. "But I am older. I am already four years old!"

Brindle laughed. "That is very old, indeed! But I think it's when you get even older that people forget how to see magic."

"But why can littler people see magic, then?" Hannah frowned. "It doesn't make sense."

"I think it's because littler people are also magic!" Brindle whispered. "It takes magic to grow into something big and amazing!"

"That does make sense," Hannah smiled. And then she frowned. "But if getting bigger means that I don't get to see magical unicorns anymore, I don't think I want to get any bigger!"

"I don't think you get a choice on whether to get bigger," Brindle told the little girl. "But you will always have the choice as to whether you want to keep seeing magic all of your life."

"Then I will make sure to always believe in magic!" Hannah announced.

"As long as you keep believing in magic, Brindle smiled, "You will always have magic in your life. I hope I get the chance to meet you again!"

"And I hope I never lose the ability to see you!" Hannah smiled happily. "I will always remember you, Brindle."

"And I will always remember you, Hannah," Brindle promised. "I will stop back and see you again sometime. Maybe we can play together."

"I would really like that!" Hannah told Brindle. "Would you like to play now?"

"I would!" Brindle said.

Brindle and Hannah spent the day playing in the sun and sand until it was time for Hannah to go home with her Mommy creature. Brindle was sad to see her go, but she knew that she and Hannah would get the chance to play again someday, and she looked forward to it.

The Unicorn and the Sun

Brindle was a magical unicorn. She was beautiful and white with a golden horn. Brindle loved to make new friends, learn new things, and to help people. These were her favorite things in the whole world!

Brindle wandered around one lazy, sunny day, and found herself in the field of flowers. She didn't see Bizzy around today, or any of her other brother and sister bees.

"Oh, bother," Brindle said. "I guess I will just have to play by myself today."

"You could play with me," a voice said from up above.

Brindle looked around to see who was talking.

"It's me, up here, in the sky," the voice said.

Brindle looked up higher, her eyes trying to adjust to the blinding light of the sun. Then she realized that it was the sun who was talking to her!

"Why, hello!" Brindle called out to the sun.

"Hi Brindle!" The sun replied.

"How did you know my name?" Brindle asked curiously.

"Why, I have heard you talking to your new friends all over the place," the sun answered.

"Why have you never said anything before?" Brindle asked.

"Because I am usually very, very busy, keeping the light all over the world until night time. Today, I am feeling a little bored. You looked bored too." The sun answered.

"Well, that's very wonderful!" Brindle said. "Well, not about the bored part, but I am very glad to meet you!"

"I am glad to finally meet you as well, Brindle," the sun said. "Do you want to do something together so that we aren't bored anymore?"

"I would very much like that!" said Brindle. "What do you want to do?"

"I don't know," the sun thought about it. "Maybe we could play some hide and seek."

"But you have nowhere to hide," said Brindle. "You are always in the sky, even when you go behind the clouds. Although, I guess that going behind the clouds would sort of be hiding. It would still be too easy for me to find you."

"That is true," the sun said sadly.

Brindle hated it when she felt anyone around her was sad. So, she thought about it for a minute. Suddenly she had an idea.

"I know!" Brindle announced. "When you go behind the clouds, and you can't see me anymore, I will hide, and you can try to find me!"

"That sounds like a perfect idea!" the sun said with a smile.

The next time that a cloud passed in front of the sun, Brindle announced, "Okay, here I go! Try and find me!"

Brindle ran quickly across the field and hid behind a tree. When the cloud passed by and the sun came out again, Brindle could feel him looking everywhere. Finally, she felt rays of sunlight slip through the leaves of the tree.

"There you are Brindle!" The sun cried out triumphantly. I found you behind the tree!"

"Very good!" Brindle laughed. "Do you want to keep going?"

"Oh, yes, please!" the sun said happily. "This is the most fun I have had in a very long time!"

Brindle and the sun spent the afternoon slipping behind clouds, and hiding until they found each other. It got a little harder as the sun kept moving and slipping down further in the day time sky.

"Well, Brindle," the sun said at last. "I think I have to leave for now. I will be back in the morning."

"I am sad to see you go," Brindle admitted. "But I know that you will be back every morning."

"I will," the sun promised. "Although most days I am busy, maybe we can play together again sometime."

"I look forward to it!" Brindle said happily as she went along her way.

(Not So) Scary Friends and Things

The Unicorn and the Nighttime Shadows

Brindle was a magic unicorn. She was beautiful, white, and had a golden horn. More than anything in the world, Brindle loved helping people, making new friends, and learning new things.

After Brindle was done playing hide and seek with the sun, and the sun was on his way home to wherever it was that he lived every night, Brindle kept wandering around, enjoying the last part of the day.

Brindle wasn't paying much attention to where she was going, or how long it took for her to get there. Before she knew it, it was dark out. Now Brindle had never really been afraid of the dark. She knew it was just a time when the sun had to take a rest to it could come out and warm the next day for play.

But today, it was a little windy. The clouds that had moved around earlier to hide the sun, now filled more of the sky. They would hide the moon for a little bit, making it even darker. The moon would peek out from behind the clouds eventually, and give a little light to the nighttime sky, and then hide again behind the clouds, making the night very dark again.

Brindle was a little nervous. She saw movement in the night, and she was a little worried.

"Who is there?" Brindle would call out whenever she saw something move in the shadows. But no one ever answered. It was making Brindle very nervous indeed.

Then the moon would come out and show a little light. Brindle was confused as to why she was so nervous.

"Am I afraid?" Brindle asked herself. "I have never been afraid before. Is this what being afraid feels like?"

Brindle wished that she could feel what she was feeling through her horn. Unfortunately, she could only feel what others felt through her magic horn, so she had to wonder what it was that she was really feeling.

Something moved again in the shadows, and it made Brindle jump. "Yes! I think I am really afraid!"

And Brindle started running. But the movement kept up with her, and she couldn't get away. She didn't understand.

"I am a magic unicorn," she said. "How can anything keep up with me?"

Then Brindle stopped and started paying close attention to the movement around her. When the moving came from over there, she looked around and saw that it was only a shadow that came from the leaves moving in the trees. It didn't look scary in the day, but it did look scarier at night.

Brindle stopped to think about it. "But the shadows of the leaves and trees aren't scary things in the day. And now that I know what they are, they aren't scary at night either!"

Brindle laughed at her own silliness. Another movement caught her eye. She turned to see what it was, and it disappeared. She was confused. She looked this way and that. Sometimes she saw the movement, and sometimes she didn't. Frustrated, she stamped her hoof down on the ground. And she saw the movement again.

Brindle laughed, suddenly realizing what it was. "It's my own shadow! No wonder I couldn't get away from it!"

Brindle stopped being afraid because she realized that all of the shadows and scary things she thought she was afraid of were really only the same things that she saw during the day. They only looked scarier at night because she couldn't tell what they were in the dark. But she knew that when the light came, from the sun, or even from the moon, that she could tell what they were, and not be afraid anymore.

Brindle laughed at herself and kept walking. She made a game up to play at night, trying to guess what each shadowy, scary thing would really turn out to be once she could see it again in the light. It helped Brindle to not be afraid of the nighttime or the shadows again.

The Unicorn and the Spider

Brindle was a beautiful, white magical unicorn with a golden horn. Brindle's favorite things in the whole world were to make new friends, learn new things, and to help people.

Brindle was walking through the woods one day when something dropped down on her nose. This startled Brindle, as she wasn't used to things dropping out of the sky and landing on her. She looked cross-eyed down her nose to see what it was, trying to focus in without shaking it off.

When she could finally focus, Brindle saw that it was a little brown creature that had landed on her nose and was now crawling around, tickling Brindle's nose. Brindle couldn't help it. She tried to stay still, but the tickling made her nose feel funny.

Prickling started inside her nose and suddenly, Brindle couldn't help it anymore. She sneezed.

"Achoo!"

The little creature hung on for dear life, staying stuck to Brindle's nose.

"Aren't you a spider?" Brindle finally was able to ask after she sneezed.

"Yes, I am," the little spider said proudly. "My name is Sadie."

"Hi, Sadie," Brindle said. "My name is Brindle. I have always been afraid of spiders. Right now, you don't seem so scary."

"I know," Sadie said with a touch of sadness. "Everyone seems to be afraid of spiders."

Brindle hated it when anyone felt sad, and she felt bad for Sadie. "I think it's because you look different from everyone else."

"Different how, do you think?" Sadie asked.

"Well..." Brindle thought about it for a minute. "You don't have eyes that are like everyone else's."

"My eyes are like everyone else's," Sadie said. "I use them to see. I have eight eyes instead of two. Some of them are because I am so little, that the extra eyes help me to see things move so that I can keep safe."

"I didn't know that," said Brindle. "But why do you have so many legs? That seems a little scary too."

"I have so many legs because I need them to help me to weave beautiful webs!" Sadie said with a smile. "Let me show you!"

Brindle watched while Sadie wove a beautiful web out of spider silk that came from out of her body. When she finished, Brindle looked at it very closely.

"That is very beautiful, Sadie!" Brindle said. "And I watched you while you were weaving. It really took a lot of work with those many legs of yours to make something so beautiful."

"Thank you, Brindle," Sadie said, blushing.

"No, thank you, Sadie," Brindle said. "Thank you for showing me something so beautiful when I was once afraid of spiders. Now I can see things in a much different way. Just because something or someone is different, it doesn't mean that they are scary. It means that they are special!"

"Do you really think that I'm special?" Sadie asked.

"Of course, you are!" Brindle said. "Can I add something to your web, so that I can be part of how special you are?"

"Oh!" Sadie said. "Of course!"

Brindle called the magic in her horn and then touched it to Sadie's web. Sparkles of magic came out of her horn and touched the web, making it shine and glitter in the sunlight.

"Oh, Brindle!" Sadie breathed happily. "You have made my web truly beautiful!"

"No," Brindle said. "I just helped make it so others could see it for how beautiful it already was."

"Well, thank you, Brindle," Sadie said sincerely. "Would you like to do some more with me?"

"I would love to!" Brindle laughed happily.

Sadie and Brindle spent the rest of the day together making beautiful, sparkling webs for everyone to see.

Monster Friends

The Unicorn and the Zesty Zombie

Brindle was a magic white unicorn with a beautiful golden horn. One day, Brindle was wandering about like she always does. Trying to learn something new like she always does. Trying to meet new friends... that was one of her favorite things to do. Then she saw something out of the corner of her eye and turned to see what it was.

And then Brindle got scared out of her skin. She screamed really loud. It was a monster.

Brindle had heard of this monster before. Brindle knew of many monsters. And she did not want to talk or approach or be around any kind of monster. So, she froze and looked away.

"eeeeexxxxccccuuuussseee meeeee." said the Zesty zombie. "Ungh, doooo youuu havvee a moooment?"

Brindle did not want to talk to a monster. That was madness and craziness. Anyways, right now she was almost too scared to talk. However, this monster did not seem to want to eat or harm her, so Brindle was finally able to get her heart to stop beating so fast.

The zombie spoke again, "IIiingh waaasss aasskskkkiiin *cough cough*." The zombie coughed and cleared its throat.

"Oh my, that is so much better. I haven't spoken in years, and there was something in my throat. It is so hard to talk when there is something in your throat. Especially when you are the undead."

Brindle gasped. This zombie was talking! That was impossible, wasn't it? Everyone knows that zombies don't talk... they just moan and groan and want to eat brains.

"You do not want to eat my brain, do you?" asked Brindle.

"Oh, that is a total myth. Zombies do not really have to eat anything. They are undead. The undead does not eat or get hungry after a while. Oh my, you are talking to me and not running away. Does that mean we are friends?" asked the zombie.

Brindle has sworn to make everyone her friend who wants to be, no matter who or what they are. So Brindle was in a bind. Friendship is the best way to learn. And Brindle loved so very much to learn.

Brindle spoke very timidly, "I will be friends with you. I am Brindle."

"That makes me very happy! I am the Zesty Zombie."

"You are Zesty?", inquired Brindle. "How can a zombie be Zesty?"

"Oh... by the way. It is very nice to meet you," Brindle finally remembered her manners.

"I am Zesty because I like to cook spicy food! Oh, it has been so long since I have cooked for anyone. You would be surprised how many others do not want to eat anything that a zombie prepares. I like to cook with some zest. So, I am the Zesty Zombie."

"Oh, that sounds, um... interesting," Brindle was hesitant. "Do you cook vegetarian? I am very much a vegetarian."

"Oh! Of course. Vegetarian food is some of my most favorite to make. Do you like red beans and rice? I make this really nummy red beans and rice dish," the zombie was starting to really get excited.

Brindle thought about the last time she had a decent dinner. Sandwiches are great, but a home-cooked meal is so wonderful.

"Okay, I will try your cooking. I like spices a little bit, but nothing too hot! Where is your kitchen?" Brindle asked.

"Wonderful!" the Zesty Zombie was getting excited. "I am a magical zombie and I have my own kitchen that I can magically create. Hang on... I have to prepare. Let's see... Beans... Onion diced... Veggie brew... and fresh-cut parsley... Oh! And the rice cooker. I love my rice cooker..."

"...all with spices," the Zesty zombie finished. "Here we go. Oh, I love to cook.!"

Brindle sat back and watched her new friend. From out of nowhere, the zombie created a full kitchen with copper pots and cupboards and a stove. A big pot of boiling water appeared from out of nowhere, and eventually, everything started to flow into it. Brindle loved that someone else could do magic too!

Then Brindle noticed that the Zesty Zombie was suddenly wearing a chef's hat. Brindle found this to be very funny but did not laugh out loud about it around her new friend, because she didn't want to hurt his feelings.

The food smelled so good!

And the spices that went into the dish. Perfection. Not too little to where it would be bland, and not too much as to where it was inedible. This zombie had some serious cooking skills.

And when the zombie was all done, he served up a bowl of white rice with red beans on top.

Brindle could not believe her nose. A veggie dish for a king, or in her case, a queen... she felt like a unicorn queen for the day!

She dug in and rolled her eyes in happiness. It was so good!

Yes, it felt a little weird having a zombie watch her eat, but Brindle knew now that this was a friend, so she was no longer scared or grossed out.

She became a very full unicorn... Brindle was full and happy.

"Oh my, I cannot eat another bite! You truly are a great and Zesty Zombie cook!" Brindle said with a smile.

Zesty Zombie smiled the most disgusting smile anyone in the history of anywhere had ever seen. It seemed that zombies did not smile well. However, Brindle saw the smile for what it was, and she smiled back.

"Normally I am afraid of monsters," Brindle told him. "But you are really nice and your food was yummy!"

"Well, if you are afraid of monsters then maybe we need to introduce you to other monsters so you are not so scared of them. What do you think of that idea? Do you want to meet some of my monster friends?"

Brindle nodded and smiled. "Of course! New adventures and more friends!"

The Unicorn and the Savvy Skeleton

Brindle and the Zesty Zombie came across a pile of bones. Brindle was a little disgusted and yet was curious as to what those bones were.

She thought, "Well, everyone is different and some people even like bones and monsters. Maybe I can try to like them too."

The bones began to click and pop when Brindle and her new friend approached.

Zesty Zombie stopped and looked at Brindle. "That is the skeleton over there in that pile. He is napping. I know you are kind of scared, so why don't we work on that... and you go over there alone."

Brindle became very scared and nervous at this point. She did not want to go over to a pile of bones by herself. But she trusted her new friend Zesty Zombie. So, she cautiously wandered over.

The bones started rattling something fierce as Brindle approached them. Popping and cracking went on for what seemed forever, before eventually, there was a yawn.

"That pile of bones just yawned," Brindle said without thinking.

And sure enough, those bones began to link together to make something... and that something was a person... and that person was a skeleton... and sure enough, that skeleton began speaking.

This surprised Brindle because skeletons do not have vocal cords.

"Who is here to wake me up?" the skeleton spoke.

"Um... it is me, Brindle. Over there is my new friend, Zesty Zombie. He brought me here to meet you."

"Oh, I forget my manners when I first wake up. I think I may be grouchy. But I am not the grouchy skeleton. I am the Savvy Skeleton. Oh... right, I need to introduce myself as well."

"I am the Savvy Skeleton."

"It's a pleasure to meet you," Brindle was still a little nervous, but her curiosity got the best of her and she just had to ask. "What makes you savvy?"

"A-hem. Yes, of course. Being savvy means that I make good, smart choices. Whenever my monster friends do not know what to decide, I always step in with my savvy abilities and help make good choices for them. Why, Miss Brindle? Do you need me to make a good choice for you?" inquired the Savvy Skeleton.

"Um..." Brindle gave it some thought and came up with something. "I am afraid of monsters. Do you think I should choose to be around them?"

"What an excellent question, Brindle! Being a monster myself, I am a bit biased on this. However, knowing monsters and what they are like so intimately, I think being around monsters is an excellent way to spend your time. Savvy?"

"Savvy," replied Brindle with a smile.

Well, this new friend was indeed not as scary as Brindle had first thought. And it seemed that he did give really good advice. Brindle gave a nod of encouragement to herself and decided the Savvy Skeleton was right.

Being around monsters was no different than being around anyone or anything else.

Then the most horrible sound came from her new skeleton friend. He was over there, cracking his knuckles!

Brindle cringed. Brindle had heard about how cracking your joints were bad for you eventually. Why would a skeleton who gave so much of himself to making good decisions make such a bad decision by cracking his knuckles?

Oh my, he is now cracking all his joints.

"Stop that," Brindle said.

"Stop what?" the Savvy Skeleton kept cracking his joints.

"Stop cracking your joints," Brindle replied.

"But it feels good! And I do what feels good." Savvy Skeleton kept cracking.

"They say that cracking your knuckles and joints eventually leads to trouble in later age. I think you are very much at a later age. Don't you think that you need to apply your ability to be savvy and see if cracking your joints is good for you or not?"

"I never gave it much thought," Savvy Skeleton admitted.

"Well, I want you to look at it, and then decide if cracking your knuckles is healthy or not," Brindle replied.

The Savvy Skeleton put his savvy skills into use. He made a face. Then he made another, completely different face. Then he looked very confused. Then he growled. Then he finally realized something.

"You are right, Brindle. Cracking my knuckles is not healthy, so I think I will stop from this day forward," he finally told her.

"You are very savvy, my skeleton friend!" Brindle smiled.

"Oh! I am your friend! You are not even a monster. I think like being your friend," Savvy Skeleton said sincerely.

And with that, Brindle now had two monster friends!

The Unicorn and the Grinning Ghost

A smoky mist started to swirl around Brindle and her two new monster friends. Brindle felt very cold. And to be honest, that thought about being afraid of monsters crept back into Brindle's mind.

Brindle was nervous, but when she looked to her new friends, they were just talking between themselves as though nothing was happening.

The mist and smoke got thicker.

Brindle felt a little scared again. This was something new, and she did not think that her new friends were aware of what was happening. Then Brindle had a thought.

What if I just calmly ask my new friends what is happening?

"Um, Savvy and Zesty, is this cold, scary mist normal?"

"Oh, that is just the ghost," said Zombie.

This did not help with Brindle's fear. She was afraid of ghosts. They were all misty and had no body to speak of. They could just pass right through her.

The thought was terrifying.

"I am afraid again, I think," Brindle said.

When her two new friends finally realized that Brindle was in a place of being afraid again, it was too late.

The most horrifying grin appeared in front of Brindle's face. It had ugly pointed teeth that looked like they could tear through anything. And it looked like they had not been brushed in years.

Brindle froze.

"Someone new," said the mouth without the smile, leaving the sharp teeth.

"Hi, Ghost," said Skeleton and Zombie together. "This is our new friend, Brindle."

This casual greeting did not help Brindle with what she saw. It was just a grinning mouth. It seemed very alarming, and all Brindle wanted to do was to make it stop!

"Help?" said Brindle. "Those teeth are mean looking. Please don't bite me!"

With that, the teeth disappeared. And then, over in the corner, the ghost started to appear. It was hunched over in a sad way. It looked down at the ground, but it was still grinning.

Brindle felt emotions coming from this grinning ghost. It was sadness.

"He is sad," Brindle said.

With this, Brindle's fear went away and she knew it was time to go into learning and help mode. It was time to put aside herself and help someone who was sad.

Brindle walked over to the hunched over ghost, "Why are you sad?"

The ghost was almost crying. "I can't stop grinning. I know my teeth are scary. I don't want them to be. I don't want to scare everyone. I am the Grinning Ghost. I can't stop grinning and I scared you with my teeth. Like I scare everyone. That makes me very sad."

Brindle looked over to the Skeleton and Zombie and realized that they felt the same.

The Ghost kept muttering about how he was always scary even when meeting new people. And that his scary teeth got in the way of making new friends.

Brindle hated it when others were sad, so she thought about it.

"I have an idea if you want some help," Brindle finally said to the Grinning Ghost.

"It would be wonderful if you could!" the Ghost said in a hopeful voice. Brindle could feel how lonely he felt.

"Well..." Brindle said slowly. "I think that your teeth are very scary. I was afraid of them. But I also think that you may need a little confidence. Your teeth make you unique and, in a way, very beautiful. Things that are different can be scary to others. When you hide in a corner because you have those teeth, you are not in a place where you can get what you want. So, let's try something okay?"

"Okay," the Ghost mumbled.

Brindle went on, "Let's pretend you are meeting me again. This time Ghost, begin at a distance further away from me. This time, let's talk at a distance first. You are going to have to take into consideration that others may need a little extra time to understand your grin."

"So, get up and let's try this again. The first thing you said to me was..." Brindle tilted her head, trying to remember. "Oh, that's right... Someone new. Say, 'someone new' again from a distance."

"I can try that," the Ghost said with hope.

The Ghost got up and swirled around. Brindle noticed that no matter what the Ghost did, he never stopped grinning. Now Brindle knew that she was about to make another monster friend. Brindle knew that this would work.

The Ghost went a little bit further away and said through his grin, "Oh, look... Someone new."

"Are you referring to me?" Brindle played along.

"I think so," the Ghost was timid.

"I am new and not a monster. I am a unicorn. It is nice to meet you! I am Brindle."

"Oh! Um... Hi... Um... What do I say now?" the Ghost was at a loss.

"Well, I think that you can start with your name and why you have that name. Then you can say that your teeth sometimes scare people and tell them to tell you if they are afraid," Brindle thought about it. "Try that."

"Okay," the Ghost started to talk. "I am the Grinning Ghost. I always grin. I know my grin can sometimes scare people. If my smile makes you uncomfortable, please let me know!"

"That was excellent! Well done!" Brindle replied. "Now I will tell you how I will reply to that."

Brindle paused. "Can I see your teeth?"

The Ghost had never been asked this question before. Even while still grinning, Brindle could tell that the ghost did not know what to do. Then Brindle thought she saw the ghost shrug, and sure enough... It wandered over.

"Okay..." said the Ghost "No one has ever really looked at my teeth before. Go ahead."

Brindle examined those sharp, scary grinning teeth. "Yes, they are extremely scary!"

But Brindle found herself not so scared. She became very curious.

"Do you have to grin all the time?" she asked.

"Yes," the Ghost replied through his scary teeth.

"Hmmm... I see. Well, my friends are accepted for who they are, no matter what they look like. I think we are friends now. What do you think?" Brindle asked.

"I have never been friends with anyone other than other monsters. I would really love to be your friend, Brindle!" the Ghost no longer seemed sad.

"Then we are friends now!" Brindle announced. "And I accept you for everything you are... including those sharp, terrifying teeth."

Brindle did not know whether telling Ghost its teeth were sharp and terrifying would help or hurt.

"My teeth are indeed sharp and terrifying," Ghost replied. "Since you accept them, Brindle, I will accept them too."

And with that acceptance of how someone looks, no matter *how* they look, Brindle now had a third monster friend.

The Unicorn and the Ridiculous Rat

"I want you to meet my friend the Rat," the Grinning Ghost was talking to Brindle.

"Hmmm... I am not a fan of rats," Brindle shivered.

"You said you wanted to get over your fear of monsters, right?" Zombie chimed in.

"Yeah, and I think it would be savvy for you to meet the Rat," Skeleton was no longer cracking his knuckles. "Look... I am no longer cracking my knuckles. Everyone can change."

With that, Brindle had to say yes. Anyways, one of Brindle's favorite words was *yes*.

"Yes... Okay, let's go meet the Rat," Brindled decided.

With her announcement, the monsters kind of giggled to themselves. They knew that the Rat was a very interesting fellow and they wondered how Brindle would become friends with such an interesting monster.

Brindle and her new friends took some time to eat some brownies that Zesty Zombie had cooked up. Well, Brindle ate some. The other monsters really did not eat, they just were polite.

The brownies were fantastic!

"You may want to save some of those brownies," said Zesty. "Rat loves them."

Brindle nodded. She wanted to eat every yummy brownie, but she knew that sharing was a wonderful way to meet someone new as well.

As the path they walked on started having more and more chewed up things, Brindle had the feeling that they were getting closer. And then...

Out jumped a Rat.

"Ridiculous!" the Rat exclaimed.

The Rat waited for someone to reply to his outburst and realized that no one was talking. So, Rat took it upon himself to talk first.

"Skeleton, you are ridiculous."

"Rat, we have been over this. I am not ridiculous. I am Savvy," Skeleton rolled what was left of his eyes. "Please stop saying I am ridiculous."

"Zombie, you are ridiculous," the Rat was at it again.

Zombie said, "Rat, you are my friend. I am not ridiculous. I am Zesty." Zombie then added, "Oh, and it is nice to see you again."

The Rat muttered something to himself about food and the zombie and smiled.

"Hi Rat!" the Grinning Ghost finally spoke up.

"Ridiculous Ghost!" the Rat went back to his routine again.

Brindle could swear that she heard the ghost sigh. Then she shrugged her shoulders and figured a misty monster was almost always sighing.

"And what is *this* ridiculous thing?" Rat was circling Brindle. "It is not a monster, and it is so ridiculous!"

"Excuse me, Mr. Rat. I am not ridiculous. I am Brindle. I am a magic unicorn and not a monster. However, that does not mean that we cannot be friends. These monsters are my new friends. Would you like to be my friend too?" Brindle asked sweetly.

"Ridiculous!" the Rat announced.

Brindle looked at the Skeleton and Zombie and Ghost. They were all smiling.

Well, the ghost is always smiling, so Brindle did not know what to make of that.

Brindle turned back to Rat. "Does that mean we are friends now?"

The Rat nodded and smiled. "You are ridiculous, Brindle. Maybe someday we can be ridiculous together."

Brindle gave this some serious thought. Being ridiculous may not be a negative thing. In fact, being ridiculous now and again could prove to be very fun.

"I would love to be ridiculous with you someday," Brindle stated. "And now we are friends!"

The Unicorn and the Misunderstood Medusa

"Let us go out for a walk. I need to stretch my bones," Savvy said.

"Ridiculous!" chimed in Rat who had somehow managed to sneak on some running shoes.

Zesty said, "I have snacks somewhere... hang on."

Brindle loved wandering around. She was all for an adventure.

"Maybe we can dance first?" asked Brindle.

"Oh, we monsters do not dance," replied Zesty.

"Well, maybe you can try it. It is fun. Let's do the cha-cha." Brindle was already finding music.

Surprisingly, all the monsters tried dancing with Brindle. Rat was a very good dancer. The Savvy Skeleton looked silly, but he was having so much fun dancing that no one really noticed.

They all started to cha-cha down the path and eventually laughed and started to wander around.

Brindle slowly began to notice statues. Stone statues of people were all around. And they all looked very afraid. Brindle thought... this is not normal... and talked it over with her friends.

"What are these statues?" She asked.

"They are people turned to stone," said Savvy.

"That's horrible!" said Brindle. "Is there nothing we can do?"

"I don't know," said Savvy. "Let's keep going and see."

Brindle didn't see any unicorns among the statues. So, she shrugged and went on. Then Brindle stopped in her tracks.

Someone was telling them to stop. Brindle didn't know what to do.

The voice finally said, "Please close your eyes."

Brindle was very curious at this point and wanted to see everything that was going on. But she did what she was told and closed her eyes.

Skeleton had an issue with this because he did not have eyelids. So, he put his boney hands in front of his eyes.

Then the voice came back. "I am so sorry. Does everyone have their eyes closed? If you see me you will turn to stone."

"This is ridiculous!" said Rat.

"Not the time, Rat. Please listen to our new friend," Skeleton urged Rat.

The voice started talking again. "Yes, I am the misunderstood Medusa. When anyone looks at me, they turn to stone. I do not know whether monsters or unicorns are immune, so I do not want to take any chances. Most of the statues you saw in the yard were people trying to cut off my head. But it seems that you're not here for that."

"Oh! We are not here to cut off anyone's head. We are just meeting new friends and learning things," said Brindle.

"Well... keep your eyes shut," said the Medusa. "I wish I could have a tea party with everyone. I just want to have tea and some friends to hang out with. All my friends turned to stone and I do not know how to fix that. I wish I did not have my powers."

"Maybe we can help. My new monster friends are very smart. Let's ask them. Zesty, Savvy, Ghost, and Rat... do you think we can help our new friend?" Brindle asked the others.

"Ridiculous!" the Rat was at it again.

"Always with the ridiculous, eh, Rat?" Zombie said. "I can't think of anything that will get rid of your special powers. Savvy... do you have any ideas?"

"Well, there is one monster that is bigger and wiser than any of us. It is very dangerous and we may get hurt. I think for our new friend we can make a go of it," Skeleton offered. "We can make a deal with the devil... The devilish dragon."

"Oh... I do not think that is a good idea," said Rat.

"What!?!? You did not say ridiculous!" said Brindle.

"Rat is right," said Zombie. "The dragon may be able to help, but it might be too dangerous."

Medusa finally spoke again. "Thank you for trying to help. I think I am always going to be cursed like this. Never mind."

Brindle did not like to give up. She could feel Medusa's sadness and hated when anyone was sad. Brindle also knew that there is always the possibility of danger when you have adventures. If it gets too dangerous, she could always walk away. She came to a determination.

"Yes, let us go see the Dragon," Brindle took charge. "Medusa do you have a way to travel?"

"I can wear my cloak pulled all over my head so that no one will see my snake hair," said Medusa.

"Snake hair... Ridiculous!" Rat said.

"Okay..." Brindle said. "Cover your head and we will guide you to the Dragon."

"Oh! I have never wandered past my home because I did not want to turn people to stone. This is very exciting! I have never traveled before," the Misunderstood Medusa said.

Brindle thought about what her life would be like if she never traveled. Just like when she met the rock. She decided that that was something that she never wanted to do. To wander and learn and meet and find new friends was too important in life to just stay at home.

Brindle knew she needed to help Medusa.

"Skeleton... You said you may know where the Dragon is. You lead us, and we will follow," Brindle was still in charge.

Medusa covered her head. Zombie and Brindle helped guide her. Skeleton led the way and Rat muttered his ridiculousness to himself. And they wandered.

To go see the Dragon.

The Unicorn and the Devilish Dragon

Brindle and her new monster friends wandered down and around and all about. Everyone was getting very tired and even though Zesty kept feeding them delicious things, they were starting to grow tired.

Skeleton kept out front, stopping continuously and looking around. He would nod and see that he had turned the wrong way and sometimes everyone had to backtrack.

This made everyone a little upset at times, but they had faith in their friend that he would get them all to the Dragon.

They rounded a curve, and then a corner, and then... there he was! Brindle had never seen a dragon before. This monster was huge!

He was also so beautiful. It looked like he was made out of metal. So shiny, with the sun glinting off of all the armored scales. He was a very intimidating beast indeed. However, Brindle was over all her fear of monsters and was ready to help her new friend, Medusa... whatever it took.

Brindle approached, getting closer and closer. She realized her first impression of this monster being huge was greatly underestimated. It was gigantic. Brindle stopped for a moment.

"No, courage is best," Brindle said under her breath and went on. Closer and closer, and then...

"Stop right there, little unicorn," the beast had a very deep voice that matched his size. "What do you want?"

"Hi... my name is Brindle. My friends over there said you might be able to help our new friend," said Brindle, only a little afraid. "I know we just met. I want you to be honest when I ask for help. I will help you in return if you need. Or maybe I can owe you a favor. I don't know. We just need help?"

Brindle realized that that was not the best introduction she had ever done, but she was very nervous. She stopped rattling on and let the dragon speak. And he did.

"Hmm..." He said slowly. "It does depend on what kind of help you are asking for. You tell me what you want and then I will tell you whether I can help you or not."

"Fair enough," Brindle nodded. "My friend Medusa, over there... well... she has this thing she does that she does not want to do."

Brindle took a deep breath and said, "She looks at someone and then they turn to stone."

The old, metallic Dragon waited what felt like a lifetime to reply.

"Hmmm..." He said at last. "I have heard of this. Medusas are very rare. And they do turn anyone or anything they look at into stone. Including you and me, Brindle. This is a very dangerous friend you have. Are you sure you want to help her?"

"Oh yes I do!" said Brindle.

"Well, I may have a solution. Miss Medusa..."

"Yes?" asked Brindle's hooded friend.

"You have snakes on your head. How many snakes are there?" the Dragon asked.

"Ummm... Ten? Wait... one, two, three, four, five..." Medusa was counting her snakes. "Twelve... Yes... Twelve snakes."

"And your eyes, assuming they turn individuals to stone, makes thirteen sets of stone making eyes."

"I think I have a solution," Dragon nodded. "I will help you, Brindle. But when I am done, I will need you to do something for me. Are you prepared to exchange help for each other?"

Brindle thought for a moment. "Yes. We can do that. I adventure all of the time. Another adventure would be a pleasure!"

"I like that attitude," said Dragon. "I need to forge some metal things for your new friend. So, everyone please stand back."

Brindle stepped back to her friends. Dragon saw they were at a safe distance and reached over to some metal rock and ripped a big chunk into its claws.

Then the Dragon began to bellow. Hotter and hotter his chest got. Finally, he coughed a bright flame into his hands where that metal was. Then Brindle saw the most amazing thing. Those huge clawed hands started to tinker and work with that hot metal. Brindle was amazed at how those big hands were making something so small!

Pounding and pounding. Working and working, that old Dragon forged and forged.

Finally, the Dragon breathed out some cold mist to cool down the metal.

"Done," the Dragon was all worked out. "Oh, by the way. I am the Devilish Dragon. Forge expert and maker of many things."

Brindle could have sworn that the Dragon was grinning.

Devilish Dragon took Medusa's hand and led her over to the new things he had created. Brindle and her friends were very curious but stayed back.

Dragon and Medusa talked and talked. Brindle watched Medusa pick up those little shiny things and stuff them under her hood.

Dragon and Medusa kept talking and Brindle overheard them trying to think about how they would know if it worked without trying it out.

It seemed that they were both very nervous about that.

Finally, Dragon decided to test his new things on himself and had Medusa look right at him. And...

He didn't turn to stone.

Brindle could feel how happy Medusa was. Dragon called them all over.

"Take a look at our new friend, Medusa," the Dragon said with a tired voice.

Brindle and all her friends saw Medusa for the first time. She definitely had snakes for hair. And...

"You put sunglasses on all her snake eyes and her eyes as well... Ingenious!" exclaimed Savvy Skeleton.

"Now why didn't I think of that?" Zombie asked, admiring Dragon's work.

"She looks ridiculous. Glasses are ridiculous!" said Rat.

"I don't think she looks ridiculous," said Brindle. "I think she looks really beautiful with her new glasses."

Medusa looked at her new friends.

And she cried. But Brindle could tell that they were happy tears. Medusa could see them, and they could see her, and she was no longer alone.

"Thank you so much!"

Everyone was very happy for her.

"Well, Brindle," the Dragon waited until everyone's excitement for Medusa settled down. "There is something that I have wanted to do for a long, long, *long* time. And it may be a very difficult journey. I hate to cut the party short, but it is time for *you* to help *me.*"

"I want a tea party," he finally announced.

The Unicorn and the Monster Tea Party

Had Brindle just heard the Dragon correctly? Did he just ask for a tea party? Isn't that what Brindle was already working on for Medusa?

Is it possible that in helping out one friend, Brindle was going to help out two new friends?

How easy!

Brindle decided to play it all cool, though. She thought that maybe if she made it an adventure, that it would be better, and much more fun than just making it easy. She wanted to include everyone, so she would give everyone something to contribute to the party.

Brindle thought and thought about each of her new friends. She wanted what they should bring to the party to be easily attainable by each of them.

And then she had it. Something all of them could bring!

"Well... it will be difficult and each one of us will have to do something for the party," Brindle smiled. "If everyone will try, I think something magical will happen."

"A tea party for the Devilish Dragon!" announced Brindle. "Is everyone ready?"

All of her new monster friends were not only very ready, but they were excited! Brindle could feel all their excitement. She knew this was going to be a win.

"Wonderful!" Brindle said. "First, we are going to need a tea set for everyone. Skeleton, can you make or find a tea set out of bone? Is this possible?"

Savvy Skeleton beamed. "I haven't made anything out of bone for a while. It would totally be fun... and my pleasure!"

Savvy ran off to get a tea set. "Be back in a while!"

"Okay... Tea set on its way. We are going to need little sweet cakes," Brindle glanced at Zombie. "Do you think you can make the most delicious little cakes and cookies and candies and sandwiches and foods for the party?"

"Yay! Of course!" Zesty was already conjuring his kitchen.

"Medusa..." Brindle addressed her new cool glasses friend. "We are going to need some music for the party. Do you like music?"

"Oh, yes! Before I was a Medusa, I was very much musical. I can get the music for the party!"

"That is most wonderful... Let me know if you need help with that!" Brindle knew it was going to happen.

"Me! Me! My turn!" exclaimed Rat.

"Oh... yes, Rat. You have an assignment. I want this tea party to be the most ridiculous tea party ever," said Brindle.

"I can do that! I am an expert at ridiculous. This will be very fun!" the Rat started to run around.

Brindle turned back to the Dragon and asked him if he wanted to do something. Since Dragons never have tea parties, he did not know what to do. So, Brindle made him very comfortable by just sitting and talking with him for the day while their new friends gathered what they would bring.

Sure enough, the Rat was the first to arrive. He had a little stage set up and it looked like he was going to do a puppet show. This amazed Brindle. He had gone way beyond her expectations. Her new friends were indeed amazing.

Then the Skeleton showed up... with a table made of bone. Oh! It was exquisite. He also had plates made of bone... a cake stand made of bone... teapots made of bone... saucers and cups made of bone... All smooth and wonderfully constructed. It was a very beautiful tea set. In fact, it was the most beautiful tea set that Brindle had ever seen!

Yet another of her friends was amazing.

Brindle went to fetch some water with the teapot. She used the magic from her horn to turn the water into tea. Now she was ready. But when she got back with the tea, she was even more amazed.

There was Medusa and her sound system. Speakers and turntables and lights... everything a dance party needed. She was playing this wonderful soft music with a good beat. It was wonderful to listen to. Medusa was at the turntables with headphones on, playing her music.

And yet another of her friends was amazing.

"Zombie... What is taking so long?", Brindle hollered to Zesty.

"I had troubles with one of the cakes," the Zombie replied.

"My friend, I think what you have is good enough. Let that one cake go and come over here and let's have some tea. You have some cakes made right?" Brindle asked.

"Yea, but I really wanted to make... this one. I am disappointed," Zesty brought over all that he had made and cooked.

Brindle's eyes popped out of her head. The things Zombie put down on the table were incredible. Pink and Purple mini cakes and all sorts of foods... so many that Brindle couldn't even begin to describe.

And yet another of Brindle's friends was amazing.

Then Brindle saw all her friends start to talk to each other. And they all came to a decision.

"We just need one more quick moment to make something, okay Brindle?" Savvy said.

"No problem," said Brindle.

All her new friends started to cook and construct and play. And then poof.

A huge cup. A huge saucer. And a huge cake appeared... Dragon sized!

"Now we are ready. Make the tea, Brindle," exclaimed Rat.

Brindle used more of her magic to make tea enough for a Dragon. The giant cup got filled. And that old Dragon sipped tea and ate pink cake.

As did everyone else.

The Rat did his puppet show and it was very ridiculous.

Music played and Medusa spun records.

Brindle laughed and enjoyed her new friends.

The tea party was a great success!

Mythical Encounters

The Unicorn and the Fairy

Brindle the unicorn was magical and very, very beautiful. She was white with a sparkling golden horn that allowed her to touch the world with magic. Brindle loved making new friends and learning new things.

One day Brindle was walking through the woods when she heard some humming. She moved to investigate the beautiful music that came from just up ahead. She followed the sound until she came to a pretty little clearing spotted with mushrooms and flowers.

A pretty little creature danced in the open area, humming and singing. When she finally noticed Brindle, she stopped.

"Oh!" the little creature exclaimed. "You are a unicorn! I have heard of your kind, but I have never seen one. It is a magical day indeed! My name is Fanny the Fairy."

"It is nice to meet you, Fanny," Brindle said sincerely. "My name is Brindle. Please don't stop... your music. It is beautiful... very magical. Fairies are magical too, are they not?"

"We are!" Fanny jumped around from flower to mushroom and back to flower again, dancing her way across the tops of the grass. "We fairies help to add beauty to the places you see in nature, touching it with the fairy magic that comes from our wings when we dance."

"I love beautiful things," Brindle told Fanny. I like to help make places beautiful too. I think everyone should get to witness beauty in their lives."

"Maybe we can do some magic together today, Brindle. And we can double the beauty for everyone to see!" Fanny said excitedly.

"Let's do it!" Brindle said. She joined Fanny in her dance, listening to the pretty music coming from the fairy and letting the golden sparkles fly out from her horn to touch all of the places around them where they danced.

Brindle and Fanny eventually grew tired and took a break. Fanny flew up and landed on top of Brindle's head, leaning against her horn to rest.

"Whew!" Fanny said. "Work can be so much fun when you do it with a friend!"

"I agree!" said Brindle. "Things are always more fun when you share it with someone else. And look at the beautiful magic we created together!"

Fanny and Brindle leaned back and admired their work. The sunny places seemed that much sunnier, and the shadows looked to be filled with muted colors of the rainbow. Even the air smelled more beautiful. The two new friends leaned back and relaxed, and just quietly shared the special place that they created together.

The Unicorn and the Will o' Wisp

Brindle was a beautiful, magical unicorn who was bright and shiny white with a sparkling golden horn. Brindle loved to go on adventures and meet new friends. She was on her way home after spending an afternoon with Fanny the Fairy, creating beautiful magical places together, when she saw a twinkling light up ahead.

Always curious, Brindle decided to investigate, to see what new things she could find. She worked her way to the spot where she saw the light, but just before she arrived, it winked out.

"Hmmm," said Brindle. "That is very curious."

Then the light twinkled again in a different place, this time from off to her right.

"Maybe I didn't go to just the right place," Brindle shrugged, and she went off to the right to follow the light. Once again, as she almost got to where the light was, it blinked out.

"Hmmm," Brindle said. "Curiouser and curiouser."

The light twinkled again, a little way up ahead and to the left.

"Let's try this one more time," Brindle said. "Now I am very curious as to what is going on."

Brindle followed the light, and once again, just before she arrived, the light winked out. Unfortunately for Brindle, as she arrived in the place where the light had past been seen, she found herself stuck in the stinky mud of a swamp.

Brindle tried very hard to pull out one hoof first and then another, but nothing worked. She was very stuck. Brindle sighed heavily. Then she heard a giggling coming from somewhere in the swamp.

"What is it?" Brindle called out. "Who's there?"

The giggling came again, this time turning into laughter.

"Hmmm," Brindle said. "I think you are not a very nice person, tricking others into the swamp to get stuck. That is actually a very mean thing to do."

"But it's funny!" A little voice said. The little sparkling light Brindle had been following winked back into view, right in front of her.

"You think it's funny to play tricks and hurt others?" Brindle asked. "Who are you?"

"I do!" the little light bounced up and down, still laughing. "And I am a will o' wisp. That is what we do. We trick people into following us into dangerous places."

"And you don't help them get out?" Brindle asked.

The little light stopped laughing and asked curiously, "Why would I do that?"

"Well..." Brindle thought about it. "I guess it could be fun sometimes to play tricks on people. But if it hurts them, then it shouldn't be fun anymore."

"I guess that's your opinion," the will o' wisp started laughing again.

"That's true," Brindle admitted. "It is only my opinion. But here... let me show you..."

Without warning, Brindle blasted a little bit of magic from her horn. The magic sparkles hit the little will o' wisp and sent it tumbling into the mud. Then Brindle used her magic to get her hooves unstuck and create a safe path on top of the swampy mud to go over to where the will o' wisp was now stuck.

"Help me!" the little light cried out. "I am all dirty, and not sparkly anymore! This is horrible!"

"Hmmm," Brindle said. "Maybe now you understand how it makes others feel when you do the same thing to them."

"I do!" the will o' wisp cried. "This is awful! I never meant to make anyone feel like this. It is a horrible thing to do!"

"Yes, it is," Brindle said. "Now let me show you what will make you feel even better than tricking someone and watching them get hurt."

"What is that?" asked the will o' wisp.

"Helping others," Brindle replied. And with that, she used the magic of her horn to pull the little light out of the murky swamp and clean it off so that it was bright and sparkling again.

"Thank you, Brindle!" the little will o' wisp jump and zipped around, happy to be free and clean again. Then it stopped in front of Brindle. "Do you really think that it makes you feel better to help people?"

"Yes!" Brindle smiled. "It is one of my favorite things to do. It really makes you feel better than a quick laugh that you might get from playing a trick on someone else."

"Hmmm," the will o' wisp thought about it. "I think the next person who follows me will find themselves in beautiful and happy places. I can help others to find hidden beauty instead!"

Brindle laughed. "That sounds perfect! I look forward to following you again one day!"

The Unicorn and the Troll

Brindle was a beautiful, magical unicorn who was bright and shiny white with a sparkling golden horn. She loved to dance and play, learn new things, help people, and make new friends! Life was always an adventure to Brindle.

One rainy day, Brindle decided to go see her friend, Brup the frog and see if he wanted to sing in the rain again. She loved an adventure, so she decided to take a different route. This route took her to the water, where there was a bridge crossing over to the place where Brup lived with his family.

Brindle went to take a step onto the bridge, and she heard a very scary voice boom out, "Halt! Who tries to cross my bridge without paying the toll?"

Brindle was surprised and stepped back off the bridge again. "I am Brindle the unicorn."

"Well, Brindle," the voice said, very scary and deep. "This is my bridge and you cannot pass without paying the toll."

"Okay," said Brindle. "What is the toll?"

"The toll is whatever is most dear and precious to you," the scary voice answered. "I think for you, that would be your horn."

"My horn!" Brindle said with surprise. "I can't give you my horn. It is a part of me. Its magic is how I can exist. Without it, I would no longer exist!"

"That is the price of the toll," the voice said.

Brindled was frustrated. "Who are you?"

"I am the Toby the troll, who always demands a toll." An ugly little creature climbed out from under the bridge.

"Well, Toby," Brindle said. "I am on my way to see a friend, and I guess I'll just have to take a different way around. I can't pay your toll."

"Well, now it's too late," the ugly little troll said. "Now you either have to pay the toll, or I will eat you."

"So…" Brindle thought about it. "My only options are to give you my horn and cease to exist, or to have you eat me and cease to exist. That sounds like two very bad choices. Either way, I will no longer exist."

"Hmmm," Toby the troll said. "You are right. I wouldn't like those choices either. But I am supposed to be a scary troll, if I back down now, then others will think I am weak, and I will never be able to collect tolls again. That sort of makes me not able to exist myself."

"So, what can we do?" Brindle asked. "It appears that we are at an impasse, but that you are willing to find another way?"

"Can you think of another way?" Toby asked hopefully. "I don't want to lose my scary image, but I also need to survive."

"Is that why you ask for tolls?" Brindle asked. "To help you survive?"

"It is," Toby admitted. "I can't really go anywhere because I can't stay out in the sunlight too long. That's why I stay under the shade of the bridge."

"Why don't you go out and do things at night, then?" Brindle asked.

"Because magic ties me to the bridge," Toby said. "If I go too far away from the bridge, then I will cease to exist."

"Hmmm," Brindle thought about it. "This is a problem."

"Yes," Toby agreed.

"Okay," said Brindle. "What if... What if I used my magic to make the bridge small enough for you to carry in your pocket? That way you could get around and do what you need, always have your bridge with you so you keep existing, and you can hide in the shade or go out at night... whatever you would like."

"You could do that?" Toby asked hopefully.

"I could," Brindle admitted. "Would you like that?"

"I would!" Toby said. "I would be free to have fun and adventures and see the rest of the world!"

"You would!" Brindle laughed. "If it's okay with you...?"

"It is!" Toby said. Then he thought about it. "But wait... first, you must cross over the bridge and get to the other side."

"Okay," Brindle said, crossing over the bridge after Toby stepped out of the way. "But why did you want me to do that?"

"Because you have just paid me the best toll ever!" Toby jumped happily.

"I'm glad to help a new friend," Brindle said with a smile. "Are you ready?"

"Oh, yes!" Toby said.

Brindle touched her magic horn to the bridge, and the bridge grew very tiny... tiny enough for Toby to pick it up and put it in his pocket, which he did. He waved at Brindle from the other side of the water.

"Thank you, Brindle!" He called out to her. "I hope to run across you again on my new life adventures!"

"I am certain that we will see each other again!" Brindle called back, and then she turned to go find her friend Brup, to sing together in the rain.

Color Friends

Brindle and the Blue Unicorn

Brindle the magical white unicorn with a beautiful golden horn was out and about, walking around as she usually did when she was out for adventure when she noticed the sky was an interesting color.

"I wonder what color that is?" asked Brindle curiously.

Confused and staring at the sky, Brindle was at a loss.

"Excuse me," said a new unicorn Brindle had never met. "I see that you are staring at the sky."

Brindle looked down from the sky at this new friend.

"Oh my," thought Brindle. "This Unicorn is the same color as the sky. Maybe he can help me figure out what color the sky is. Maybe I should not ask him to help? It is not always easy to ask for help?"

"Hi," said Brindle. "I am looking at the sky and I see that it is the same color as you are. May I ask, what color are you?"

"Of course, I will tell you my color!" said the unicorn. "I am always happy to help and share, it makes me feel good to help others. I am the color Blue."

"Blue, huh?" said Brindle. "I am trying to learn what colors are because I think I like colors. You are my first color. It is nice to meet you, Blue Unicorn. Is that your name?"

"Yes, we all share the color names so that we can all be together. I love the color Blue, and I am very glad it is your first color that you have learned. There are many different colors and I can introduce you to them if you want." The Blue unicorn said.

"That would be wonderful!" said Brindle. "But I have more questions before we go to meet your friends. Like... what is the color blue?"

"That is my favorite question to answer!" said the Blue Unicorn. "Blue is one of three primary colors in painting and nature. With the science of nature, Blue lies between violet and green on the spectrum of light. Your eyes see blue when it is observing light between 450 and 495 nanometers."

"*That* is Blue," the Blue Unicorn said proudly. "What do you think about what I just said?"

"That is very confusing and complicated," said Brindle. "I am not sure I understand what you just said. I know! I can use my horn on you to see what blue is... maybe that will be easier."

"My horn makes things turn blue. What does your horn do?" asked the Blue Unicorn.

"It tells me what emotions are, among other things," said Brindle. "I like to ask permission before I use my horn on someone. May I try it on you?"

"Of course! Be my guest!" said the Blue Unicorn.

Brindle powered up her horn and began to see the color blue in connection with her new unicorn friend.

"It is interesting that most people associate sadness to the color Blue," said the Blue Unicorn. "That is not entirely true. I look forward to seeing what your horn sees."

Brindle relaxed and let the color blue swim around her. "Oh my, this is a very boy color. Boys normally are thought of as blue. And look... deep blue is a very powerful color when it comes to working. This color has much depth and stability. It is trusting with intelligence. Oh, I like this color!" said Brindle.

Then Brindle turned her horn on even more. Oh... light blue is the color of the sky, whereas dark blue makes you feel very serious thought. This is a very stable emotion I am feeling.

"Blue is a very wonderful color!" announced Brindle. "It is very intelligent and stable."

The Blue Unicorn puffed up his chest with pride and his horn glowed.

"Oh, thank you very much! That is very much how I feel. I am very proud to be stable and smart. Thank you, Brindle. You are my new friend and you make me feel good. I hope your horn can tell that I am very happy."

"It does!" Brindle smiled.

"Shall we meet my other friends of color? I am sure they will really like meeting you. And you can use your horn on all of them to see what they are like. This is very interesting... You are a very interesting unicorn, Brindle."

Brindle powered down her horn and smiled. She liked to make new friends... so how could she say no? Anyways, she really did not have much to do today other than learning and adventuring... and learning is the best.

"It would be my pleasure to meet your friends!" said Brindle.

"Then off we go! Follow me," the Blue Unicorn replied.

Brindle and the Red Unicorn

"Let us see all the primary color unicorns first," said the Blue Unicorn. "Red is a primary color. Although this is not to say that one color is more important than any other color. All the colored Unicorns are equal here. No one color is more important than another. It is just when you paint in the real world, some colors are primary and some secondary because some colors can be mixed together to make new colors. Blue, Red, and Yellow are primary colors because that is where colors start. Not because they are more important."

"You like to talk, don't you, Blue Unicorn?" laughed Brindle. "I like that. I do not always understand what you are saying, but you keep talking, because I think it makes you happy. And I want you to be happy."

"I know I like to talk. Thank you, Brindle, for making me feel okay with talking a lot. It makes some unicorns uncomfortable with how much I say all the time. I do tend to ramble most of the day. It just kind of keeps flowing out of me I think," the Blue Unicorn stopped talking because he realized he was doing it again.

"I am talking too much again," he said.

"Not at all!" said Brindle. "You are my friend and you can talk as much as you want to. I like you for who you are."

"That's really a great attitude, Brindle. I like you too," the Blue Unicorn smiled. "Now let's go meet the Red Unicorn."

Brindle was not ready for what she saw. Red was such an amazing color! When she saw the Red Unicorn for the first time, Brindle's eyes went so wide they almost popped out of her head. What a majestic unicorn the Red Unicorn was! So vibrant... and it looks like it could run so fast. Red seemed like a very fast color.

"Hello, Red Unicorn," said the Blue Unicorn. "Meet my new friend, Brindle."

The Red Unicorn smiled and winked at Brindle. Then Brindle saw the Red Unicorn turn and look down at the ground... and it glowed!

The Red Unicorn was glowing! Brighter and brighter until Brindle just had to ask, "What are you doing?"

"I am showing you my favorite red," said the Red Unicorn. "It is called pink."

The Red Unicorn kept glowing in front of Brindle, getting more and more bright with white light.

"Look at this, Brindle... When you make red bright with white light, it becomes pink. The more and more white energy I put into me, the more I become so beautiful and pink."

The Red Unicorn calmed down and began to stop glowing until it was back down to its original red.

"That was so wonderful!" said Brindle. "How do you do that?"

"My horn is more than just the making of red," said the Red Unicorn. "It makes the best color in the world when I concentrate... pink."

"Oh! I like pink very, very much," said Brindle. "I wish *I* was pink."

"You want to be pink?" asked the Red Unicorn. "I can do that, with your permission. It will only last a little while and then it will wear off. Would you like to be pink for a while?"

"Oh, yes! Very much so!" Brindle was excited.

The Red Unicorn's horn lit up and then she pointed her horn right at Brindle. "Here we go... this may tickle a bit, so giggles are totally allowed."

Brighter and brighter Brindle felt. She looked down at her body and it was glowing too. It did indeed tickle! Was all pink ticklish?

"This is a wonderful sensation!" She said. And then all of a sudden, Brindle's color changed.

Brindle was now the color pink! Brindle's chest puffed up and she felt so very good as a pink unicorn.

"How do I look?" Brindle asked.

"Wow..." said the Blue Unicorn. "I think I am speechless."

"Well that is saying something now is it not?" Brindle laughed.

"I think you look exceptionally beautiful!" said Red Unicorn. "Everything needs to be pink. Don't you think?"

"I think everything needs to be blue," said Blue Unicorn.

"Can't we all just share our colors?" asked Brindle.

"It is very interesting that you say that, Brindle," rambled Blue Unicorn. "When Red Unicorns and Blue Unicorns combine, they make a secondary unicorn. Maybe Red Unicorn and I can open the portal to the world of secondary colors and then you can see what happens when red and blue combines."

Red Unicorn rolled her eyes. "You do speak a lot, Blue Unicorn. But he is right. Purple is a color you need to meet eventually, Brindle. However, are you all not meeting the primary colors first? Have you met my friend, Yellow Unicorn?"

"What is the color Yellow?" asked Brindle.

"Come with me and we will go meet her," said Red Unicorn. "See if you can keep up... red is a very fast color!"

She was right. Brindle and Blue Unicorn had a very hard time keeping up with the Red Unicorn. Brindle thought that Red Unicorn slowed down for her a few times. But that is what friends do. They slow down for each other so that everyone can be together. As Blue Unicorn and Brindle panted and ran, Red Unicorn circled and giggled and laughed and kept her new friends happy while they traveled.

Brindle and the Yellow Unicorn

Brindle started to feel a warm glow. This was not the glow of intense pink. That color had finally worn off. Brindle felt a little bit of sadness about losing her pink color and yet was very excited to meet a new color. Anyways, she had a new friend and knew that all she needed to do was ask Red Unicorn to make her pink again and it would happen.

That was the beauty of friends. They ask and know what each other wants and then they help out.

Brindle saw the area around her change and glow golden. This new color seemed to be even more abundant than the color blue of Blue Unicorn.

And there was the new friend she came to meet... she was beautiful and glowing and shining with a warm light. Brindle saw that this new unicorn almost looked like it was metal. Brindle knew what metal was, and that it was shiny and smooth.

Then Brindle stopped and realized her new friends were behind her.

"Why did you stop?" asked Brindle.

"You go ahead and meet Yellow Unicorn. We will stay here... right, Blue Unicorn?" the Red Unicorn told Brindle.

"Absolutely! Meeting a new friend on your own can be tough, but sometimes it is nice to approach someone new and try to meet them. This is a very hard thing for the mind and body to do, especially when someone is introverted. I do not think you are introverted, Brindle. But sometimes it is cool to meet someone new as just yourself to not scare or intimidate them."

"Oh my..." Brindle thought to herself. "The Blue Unicorn is talking a lot again." Brindle did not understand much of what he said about being introverted and stuff. Maybe she could wink and smile at Blue Unicorn so that he knows that friends support each other.

Brindle winked and smiled. Blue Unicorn smiled back.

"Ok, time to meet a new color unicorn," announced Brindle.

Brindle wandered over to the new unicorn. Brindle attempted her best approach. Head up with a nice smile, combined with kind eyes and a slow approach often worked best when meeting someone new. Also, having confidence helped.

Brindle did all these things and more, and her best efforts paid off. She did not even have to talk first.

"Hello," said Yellow Unicorn.

"Hello," replied Brindle.

"I see you are hanging out with Red and Blue Unicorn," Yellow Unicorn said. "They are my friends, and if they are friends with you that means that we can become friends too! A Yellow Unicorn is what I am. What do you think of that?"

"It is very nice to meet you," Brindle smiled. "I am Brindle."

The Yellow Unicorn went back to munching on its lunch. Yellow was a very interesting color.

"Hmmm..." said Brindle to get Yellow's attention. "I am learning about color and my friends tell me you are a primary color. Can you tell me what yellow is?"

"You want to know what yellow is? Well... well... Hmm... That means I have to think of what I am. That may not be easy. It is not easy to know who and what you are," said the Yellow Unicorn. "But for you, Brindle, I will try."

"Why thank you, so kindly!" replied Brindle.

Yellow Unicorn thought and thought about what it means to be yellow. The sun was yellow. Well, white actually. Yellow Unicorn does not really like to identify with anything and the moment they do, they forget so that they can go back to not identifying.

"I am not sure how to describe yellow, Brindle. I am at a loss," the Yellow Unicorn went back to her thing.

"Oh... Okay," said Brindle, a little disappointed.

Brindle thought... "This is indeed a very interesting character." And then Brindle realized... her horn... she could use her horn!

"Um... Yellow Unicorn?" Brindle said shyly. "I can use my horn to tell us what your color is. My horn is very special for it sees emotions connected to things. I can only use it with permission. Do I have your permission to see what yellow is with my horn?"

"Hmm... That is very interesting," replied Yellow Unicorn. "I do not see the harm in it. All things can be tested and checked out... including me. Go ahead!"

Brindle got all excited. It seemed that these new friends of hers were very nice. Her horn charged up and Brindle began to work her magic.

"Oh! I see many things now!" Brindle said in awe. "Yellow is the color of sunshine and happiness. It is a very hopeful color. And look... yellow can be freshness and happiness. It is a positive color and very clear with energy and optimism. And, oh! Look... it is also a representing color for cowards and intelligence."

"You are a great many things, Yellow Unicorn," Brindle said solemnly.

The Yellow Unicorn pondered Brindle's words and nodded her head. Indeed, yellow was a very multi-purpose color. The Yellow Unicorn was very pleased with Brindle's assessment.

And then she promptly forgot everything Brindle said. "Did you get your answer, my new friend Brindle?" she asked innocently.

"Oh, indeed I did," said Brindle with a smile.

Blue and Red Unicorn came over to where Yellow Unicorn was. They exchanged play and friendly greetings and ran around chasing each other. Brindle just smiled as her new friends ran around and around. Then she noticed something. As her colored friends ran about, they glowed... and the light behind them began to combine with other lights. Yellow was combining with blue and blue with red, and so on. It was amazing to see for sure!

And then something amazing happened.

Pop.

A new unicorn appeared.

Brindle was shocked and very happy at the same time. It seems that when primary colors combine, they make new colors. Brindle wondered what this new color was.

All of the unicorns stopped playing and gave hugs to the new unicorn in the center.

Brindle and the Purple Unicorn

This new color of unicorn very much sang true to Brindle's heart. It was such a wonderful color! And look how royal it was! Maybe it was a rare color? It seemed to be calm and intense at the same time.

Brindle watched and watched and watched.

And then Brindle felt something that she did not like. She felt alone. She did not have a color and all the other unicorns were playing and she was just watching.

Watching is okay, but Brindle wanted to play too. The other unicorns were talking with this new unicorn and Brindle became rather lonely.

She did not like being lonely, so...

Over to the unicorns she went. Now, Brindle did not have color yet. She looked down at herself and did not see any color like these unicorns were. Maybe she did not belong or fit in with the color unicorns because she had no color?

As Brindle thought and thought to herself about not fitting in, she wondered what to do about it. Maybe she should just stay quiet and be by herself while her new friends played. Maybe she was different and will never fit in because she had no color.

Then again... Maybe being different was okay after all. When she gave it some serious thought, she realized that being different is a wonderful thing!

This gave Brindle new confidence. She was very different from the color unicorns. This made her feel a little left out. However, Brindle had great pride in herself. This confidence gave Brindle an idea. Maybe she can talk to the other unicorns about how she did not have any color and felt like she did not fit in.

Brindle went over to talk to her new friends about her feelings.

"Hi there! You all playing together is wonderful to watch," Brindle smiled shyly.

The other four Unicorns just stared at Brindle.

"Thank you?" said the Red Unicorn.

Brindle gathered the courage to speak. It was very hard to talk to others about how you feel. Feelings are different for everyone. Brindle's horn tells her *that* all the time.

Brindle looked at the ground while she talked. "Ummm... I got lonely over there watching you play. And... I... I was wondering what your thoughts were about it. You see, I have no color and I feel like I do not fit in with everyone playing. Am I an outsider? I don't know. What do you think?"

Blue Unicorn got really sad and stepped forward.

"Oh, Brindle. We are sorry," Blue Unicorn looked at the Yellow, Purple, and Red Unicorn. They nodded as Blue Unicorn spoke again.

"We didn't think about how you have no color. It does not matter to us. We are your friend and you are our friend and we like that you are different than us."

The Blue Unicorn looked at the other unicorns and they all nodded in agreement.

Blue Unicorn went on, "Now, Brindle... Come play with us and then we will introduce you to our newest friend, Purple Unicorn. You know how to run, don't you? Come run with us!"

Red Unicorn took this as a moment of pride and ran circles around Brindle! Zoom! Zoom!

Then they all started to run again. They all ran and ran until they fell over and laughed.

Yellow Unicorn spoke. "Brindle, this is Purple Unicorn. It is the complimentary unicorn color to mine."

Blue Unicorn just had to speak. "There is a color wheel where all the colors are represented. There are colors that complement and contrast each other. When colors are exactly opposite on the wheel, they complement each other when they are put together. One would think that colors so opposed would not fit well together but they do!"

Red Unicorn stopped Blue Unicorn. "Blue, just say they work well together."

Blue nodded his head. "Yes, Purple and Yellow work well together. They complement each other."

Purple Unicorn finally spoke, "Hey, do not talk like I am not here. Ask me! I know what color I am."

Brindle felt part of the group again. She relaxed even though there was still this feeling inside of her that she had no color. That could be discussed later. What she needed to look into now was to learn what this new color unicorn was.

"Hello, Purple Unicorn, she introduced herself. "I am Brindle."

"Woot!" said the Purple Unicorn. "My color is one of royalty but I don't like being royal. I like being bratty. So, woot!"

Purple Unicorn ran around Brindle and encircled her with a lovely lavender glow. Brindle could smell herbs and wonderful smells. It was so relaxing. When the Purple Unicorn slowed down to a trot, all the other Unicorns inhaled deeply smelling the sweet scent of lavender.

"Oh! That is very relaxing and wonderful!" exclaimed Brindle.

Looking around, Brindle saw that the other Unicorns were very relaxed as well. Purple was a wonderful color. Brindle thought about where she had seen Purple in nature... and she thought of flowers.

"Oh! These flowers I see all the time are, in fact, purple," stated Brindle.

"Yes! I do that. I make flowers purple with my horn. It is my specialty." Purple Unicorn did a little dance. "I also make some gemstones my color too. They are very rare though."

"Purple gemstones... How interesting!" replied Brindle.

Brindle thought about using her horn on this new unicorn to see what emotions purple made but decided to spend time with her new friend just hanging out. And in having a little patience, something very wonderful happened.

"Brindle, want to see me do something neat?" asked the Purple Unicorn.

"Oh, yes!" Brindle said.

The Purple Unicorn began to do its dance. Then it began to vibrate. Faster and faster, more and more, it vibrated. Round and round. Dance and dance. Vibrations built up so intensely until Brindle could barely look at Purple Unicorn. And then...

Blam! A purple light burst out of Purple Unicorn and made everything around them purple, all at once. Red became Purple. Blue became Purple. Yellow became Purple... and Brindle as well.

Then Brindle felt something that was very wonderful.

She felt creative. And she wanted to make something. To color and write and design and be creative. She wanted to do something creative for her home and her world and her friends. This feeling of creativity was indeed very, wonderful!

Red Unicorn made creative red footprints on the ground

Blue Unicorn began to speak poetry out loud.

Yellow Unicorn just glowed so softly and warm.

Purple Unicorn smiled and said to Brindle, "That is my other talent. Giving my color for others to be creative with. Whenever you get stuck on a drawing or being creative, just add my color and normally it opens you up to be creative."

"Yes, I do feel very creative! This is very wonderful," Brindle remarked.

"Well... then I think it's time you meet the other two secondary colors. EVERYONE RUN!" Purple Unicorn called out happily.

The creative process combined with the running of colors made a whirl around Brindle. Brindle ran too, and she changed color so many times she didn't know what color was what. She even began to understand that she did not have to have a color to be happy. And then.

Pop.

Pop.

Two new Unicorns.

Everyone stopped.

Brindle and the Green and Orange Unicorns

Brindle was always amazed at how these color unicorns made new friends. Brindle did not understand where these new colors were coming from and yet felt very relaxed in the fact that new colors happen all the time.

These two new colors started to make Brindle's head spin. Yellow and Blue and Red Unicorns were hard enough to remember. Now there were Purple and two new unicorns.

That was six unicorns in all very different colors. How complicated!

Then Brindle relaxed and realized that sometimes things do get complicated. When we get worried about complicated things, nothing ever gets done. And Brindle wanted to get things done. She wanted to learn about new colors. And she knew that when things get complicated to break them down into simpler, more easily handled parts.

She decided to work on the complicated mixtures of unicorn colors. Brindle puffed up her chest and straightened her horn. "Well, let's get to work!" thought Brindle. "Complicated or not, we have new friends to meet. I always try my best. So here goes..."

Brindle started to talk to these two new unicorns but was too late. They were already jumping around and talking.

"I am Green," pranced the Green Unicorn.

"I am Orange... nothing rhymes with me," professed the Orange Unicorn.

"You're right... nothing rhymes with orange. There are poetry experts who are very amazed that nothing rhymes with orange. We are at research and scientific loss about the color orange rhyming with anything," Blue Unicorn kept talking until he mumbled into the corner, happily talking to himself.

"Yes, I am unique," stated Orange Unicorn.

Yellow Unicorn stepped up. "Hang on... hang on Green and Orange! You need to meet our new friend Brindle before you start talking about yourselves."

"Oh, yes we do!" said Orange Unicorn

"Hi, Brindle," both Orange and Green said together.

Brindle smiled. She did now feel like she was special... like all these other unicorns. Now that she was accepted by them, she no longer felt like an outsider. Brindle found her own strength within herself and did not need anyone to tell her she was special. Brindle knew it.

"So, you are Green and you're Orange... am I right?" asked Brindle, pointing first to Green and then to Orange.

Both of the new unicorns nodded.

"Two colors at once is a little overwhelming!" stated Brindle. "Maybe I can learn each of your colors individually."

All of Brindle's new friends nodded at her wisdom and bravery to take on colors.

"Let's do me first then!" stated Orange Unicorn. "Orange is a combination of Red and Yellow. Orange is a very successful color. If you cannot tell, I am a very enthusiastic unicorn. I love to be excited about things! I also like to encourage others. I find myself to be very attractive. Do you all think I am attractive?"

The other unicorns nodded in agreement. Orange was indeed an attractive unicorn. Then again, all unicorns are beautiful.

"That is very interesting," stated Brindle. "I think I can see how combining Yellow and Red can make a unicorn like you. I do also know that you are your own unicorn. Orange, you are *very* attractive."

The Orange Unicorn beamed and glowed. Then Brindle looked at the other unicorn, the Green one, and saw something very peculiar. The Green Unicorn was pointing its horn at the ground and a little plant was growing. And it was growing at the same color as the unicorn pointing its horn at it.

The little plant grew and grew until it was the same size as the unicorn itself.

"Ummm... Purple, can you put a little color on this?" asked the Green Unicorn. "I grew it with my color and it now needs a little of your color, I think."

"My pleasure! Of course! Right away!" Purple Unicorn pointed its horn.

Brindle sat back and watched with amazement. She watched as the Purple Unicorn pointed its horn at each and every flower on the Green Unicorn's plant and they changed into the most beautiful purple.

This was amazing! Could unicorns combine colors with more than just themselves, running around in circles? It seems that they could. In fact, it was happening right in front of Brindle!

The flowers on the Green Unicorn's plant were changing purple. And then a very interesting thing happened. All the unicorns started to use their horns to change the colors of the flowers. Some combined and changed the colors of the stems of the plants, turning them into a dirt color. Some made orange flowers and yellow flowers and all the colors started to combine.

Blue Unicorn just watched and nodded. It was like he was just watching and learning how the unicorns combine color. Every now and again he would offer suggestions, but allowed all the other unicorns to paint the flowers all the colors they wanted.

Green Unicorn wandered over to Brindle. "Sorry about that. Sometimes I just have the creative urge to grow something."

"That is very understandable," said Brindle. "I think growing things is much better than destroying them."

The Green Unicorn made a face and nodded in agreement. Green Unicorn only grew things. So, what Brindle said about creating and growing, Green Unicorn totally understood. There was something else Green Unicorn wanted to do to show off to Brindle but it waited to see what Brindle wanted to see first.

"How big can you grow something?" asked Brindle.

This was the question Green Unicorn wanted to hear. In fact, he was about to grow something really big to show off to Brindle. He was glad he waited.

"I have grown a great many things!" Green bragged. "Some as tall as the sky... Trees that are so big you cannot wrap your hooves around them. I think that I could show you how that works. However, I think the other unicorns will get impatient while I do that. It takes a really long time to grow something that big."

Brindle nodded and learned. Growing things was something that Brindle wanted her horn to do. Feeling emotions was awesome, however, Brindle wanted to grow things. She supposed she would have to do it like everyone else and use dirt and seeds.

"So, color connects you all?" asked Brindle.

"Yes," said the Green Unicorn. "Color connects the world!"

"That is so wonderful!" Brindle was excited to be with her new friends.

Brindle and the Day of Color

"So, hang on... watch this," the Blue Unicorn painted the sky and the land and everything the darkest of darkest blue. "Brindle... let's all have a day of color. And the day starts with a night. The contrast in anything makes art and they say that sunrise is one of the most artistic things to color."

Blue Unicorn worked and worked and worked until almost everything was covered in blue-black. He left a few holes in the sky allowing them to be stars. The Blue Unicorn really knew that stars were giant balls of flaming material, but did not want to talk about that while he was working so hard on making everything blue-black.

Finally, the Blue Unicorn stepped back with his friends and announced that the day was about to begin.

All the other unicorns got ready by powering up their horns and they smiled at Brindle.

"A day of color," said the Blue Unicorn. "Now I will bring up the blue with some white energy."

A glow began at the horizon, where the sky met the ground. It was a little bit of light blue. Blue Unicorn kept quiet about the science behind daylight and just brought in some light.

"I will keep making the sky lighter blue..." Blue Unicorn said instead. "Everyone can paint now."

All the unicorns began to paint the sky. Yellow started and Orange followed. Purple played amongst the edges and even Green got into the mix and put in some color. Red Unicorn danced and danced and ran and ran, putting red on everything.

Yellow eventually came in and changed the sky from red to orange to yellow to white. All the while, orange also ran with red, changing colors as red went running around.

All the while, Blue intensified the white energy in the blue sky.

When they were all done, the sunrise was complete and they all gave each other hugs, including Brindle.

Brindle found that she was speechless. This was indeed the best sunrise that she had ever seen in her life. It was amazing! Brindle could have stared at this sunrise all day, but someone interrupted her.

"Ummm..." it was Blue Unicorn again, seeming a little shy and not wordy for once. "Do you like it?"

"I am speechless!" said Brindle. "It's beautiful! It's... just wow!"

"Do you want to stare at this, or do you want to see what else we can color today?" asked Blue.

"Oh... right! Better to learn and move about. Good idea Blue Unicorn!" Brindle was still looking at the sunrise.

So, Blue went over to the other unicorns and began to have a little chat. They all nodded eventually and all came over to see Brindle. Orange Unicorn spoke.

"We have decided to color all day for our new friend, Brindle. We want to color what you want to color Brindle. So, you tell us what you want to work on and we have all agreed to color what you want."

This was quite the gift for Brindle. A coloring book of magical unicorns was the best way to color anything in this world! Brindle took a moment and thought about what she really liked.

Well, she liked candy and hugs and all the wonderful stuff that makes a person happy. However, she thought that coloring a hug maybe a bit too difficult for her new friends. So, she thought about the world and figured out what she liked.

"I like the ocean," Brindle just spoke that without thinking.

"Oh, the ocean is Green's and my most favorite!" said Blue Unicorn.

"There are even Purple things in the ocean. Think of all those colorful fish and coral," said Purple Unicorn.

Red spoke up. "I think every color is in the ocean. Good idea, Brindle! And maybe we can clean up the ocean while we color it."

Everyone had a plan now and was ready to work. They were all excited and Purple Unicorn powered them up with creativity.

Blue and Green Unicorn had the hardest job because they had to color all the water. This work made them very happy because they loved to work hard.

Purple and Red and Yellow and Orange all started in on the seashells and fish. A smattering of color and paint went everywhere.

"Oh... this is wonderful!" said Brindle.

This encouragement made the unicorns work even harder. They painted the sand and the grass and the rocks and the coral and even got together to talk about coloring the really deep animals in the ocean.

The unicorns kept all the life in the ocean safe and clean while they worked. They all cleaned and painted and worked and danced and ran and had fun until the entire ocean was painted every color of the rainbow.

And it was noon.

"I think we need to break for lunch," said Brindle. "Maybe we can have some peanut butter sandwiches. I can always make lunch with my magic for more than just me. We can share my lunch!"

All the unicorns were starving and every bite of every sandwich was like magic! When they were done eating, they all looked at Brindle again.

Brindle felt the pressure of the next coloring assignment. But she knew she was up to the task. She only had to just blurt out what she liked and then they will paint it.

"I like national parks," stated Brindle.

"My word, Brindle. You are a very special unicorn! We love... and we mean *love*... national parks. They are so beautiful!" said the Purple Unicorn.

"Let's paint them all today!" said the Orange Unicorn.

Everyone nodded in agreement and got to work.

Mountains and plains and water and lakes and trees... oh so many trees... were painted. Deserts and cactus and colored mountains. Rivers and green fields... and flowers everywhere!

Those unicorns painted jungle reserves and swamp reserves and snowy polar reserves and, well, every park in the world all the way down to the park near Hannah's house with the playground and everything.

"Whew!" said Brindle. "That was a whole lot of work, and quite a busy afternoon. I think we did a magnificent job!"

All the unicorns were starting to get very tired. But they all agreed with Brindle that they had done a magnificent job. They were all tired, but they knew they had to do one final coloring for Brindle.

A sunset.

Blue Unicorn began to darken the sky. And Yellow and Orange began to paint everything around Brindle. Red came behind them and began to paint as well.

Green and Purple started to change all the greens and purples into darker and darker greens and purples.

Orange Unicorn painted everywhere. Yellow started to slow down. They were about done for the day.

Green and Purple finally came back and realized that they were as dark as they can go until Blue did his thing.

Blue kept going, allowing every other color to paint over his color Blue.

Finally, Orange came and sat down next to Brindle. "It is up to Red and Blue to finish out the sunset."

Brindle watched as even Red retired from coloring. Finally, it was just Blue and he made blue darker and darker and darker with some pinholes of white stars in the night sky. Blue walked over to Brindle, tired but happy.

"Well, Brindle. What do you think of colors?" he asked.

"I love you all so much! And if I had to pick a favorite color, it would be... *All* of you. You are *all* so beautiful!" Brindle made sure she made eye contact with all the unicorns.

They all smiled and laughed and faded into the night, leaving Brindle with a lovely, warm night sky.

"Bye, Brindle!" all of the unicorns said at once. "We love you too!"

And the colors faded into nighttime.

Extra Unicorn Adventures

The Unicorn and the Sad Child

Brindle the magic unicorn was a happy little adventurer who loved to make new friends and have adventures, learning new things.

One day, Brindle was walking along the edge of a neighborhood and came across a playground where there were all kinds of things for children to play on and have fun. The thought of children like her friend Hannah playing and having fun made Brindle smile.

Then she felt a sadness coming from someone in the playground. Brindle looked around to see if she could find where the sadness was coming from. And she did. Hiding in one of the playground toys was Hannah, her human child creature friend from the beach. But Hannah looked very, very sad.

Brindle poked her head in through the hidey-hole where Hannah had tucked herself away and blew some sparkles from her horn in Hannah's direction. "Why are you so sad, Hannah?"

"Oh, Brindle!" Hannah cried. She stuck her foot out toward Brindle. "I have something stuck to my foot and I can't get it off!"

Brindle looked closely and saw what the problem was. There was a sticky piece of paper clinging to the bottom of her shoe. Brindle gently touched her horn to the paper and pulled it off from Hannah. The only problem now was that it was stuck to Brindle's horn!

"Oh, Brindle!" Hannah laughed and crawled out of her hidey-hole. She reached out and grabbed the piece of paper off of Brindle's horn. "Thank you, Brindle. I have missed you."

"I was just thinking about you, Hannah," Brindle said with a smile. "Here, let me make that go away with my magic."

"Silly," Hannah said. "That is a wonderful thing, but you don't have to be magic to take care of this."

Hannah took the piece of paper, crumpled it up and walked over to a garbage can on the playground and threw the paper in.

"You're right!" Brindle said. "You don't have to be magic to do that!"

Brindle looked around the playground, noticing the garbage all over the place. Pieces of paper, wrappers, plastic, and soda cans were crumpled all over, making the playground look not so fun after all.

"Is the trash the reason that kids don't come here to play anymore?" Brindle asked.

"I think so," Hannah said sadly. "I never see kids come here anymore."

"Then maybe we can clean this place up and children can come to find the magic here again!" Brindle offered.

"Really, Brindle?" Hannah asked. "That would be wonderful!"

"Then let's get started!" Brindle laughed.

She and Hannah spent the rest of the afternoon cleaning up all the mess on the playground that careless people had left behind. When they were done, Brindle and Hannah sat together on the merry-go-round, gently turning to see all of the cleaning they had done.

"It looks wonderful, Brindle!" Hannah said happily. "Thank you so much!"

"Of course, Hannah!" Brindle smiled. "I love to help my friends. And maybe now you can make some new friends."

Brindle pointed her horn to where some children were coming to look at the now clean playground. "You go meet them and I will come by again and see you again someday."

"Thank you again, Brindle!" Hannah gave Brindle a quick hug and ran off to make some new friends with the children in her neighborhood.

Brindle smiled and left, but checked back every once and a while to watch the children play. It was the kind of magic that was better than any other... the magic of friendship and play!

The Unicorn and her Special Day

Brindle was a very special unicorn who loved meeting new people, helping others and learning new things. She was beautiful and white, with a golden horn. Best of all, Brindle was magic!

One day Brindle was walking around, thinking about all of the adventures she had recently had, and all of the new friends she had made. It had been quite the adventure lately!

It was a bright sunny day, and Brindle paused for a moment to feel the warmth of the sun, and feel the fresh breeze in the air. She reached out with the magic of her horn, and she felt... happy! It was strange, but a good feeling. The happy wasn't coming from her, but she could feel a big happy coming from somewhere nearby. Someone was very, very happy. The thought made Brindle smile, and then she laughed with the pure joy of it.

"I love happy!" Brindle said. "Happy is the best thing in the whole world!"

When she opened her eyes, she saw a light flash in the trees. That had to be the will o' wisp. It was fainter right now in the daylight, but she was sure that was him. So, Brindle decided to wander over in his direction.

Just like when she first met him, when she came close to where he was, the light winked off.

"Yay!" Brindle said to herself. "Someone who wants to play! I hope he's keeping true to his word and only taking people to beautiful places."

Brindle saw the light appear again, still faint in the sunlight, but bright enough for her to see.

"Let's play along," Brindle said, and she once again followed the will o' wisp. Brindle was a little excited. "I wonder what beautiful place he is taking me to?"

Brindle followed the will o' wisp through the trees, blinking first in one place and then turning off and blinking in another place, leading Brindle on a new adventure. She could feel the happy feeling growing, getting closer, and she became even more excited.

Finally, the will o' wisp took her to the rock she had met before, on the edge of the trees next to the field of flowers.

"Hello, Mr. Rock," Brindle smiled happily.

"Hello, Brindle!" the rock replied. "It is very nice to see you again."

"I agree!" Brindle said. "Are you friends with the will o' wisp? I think he brought me here to see you. Did you need something?"

"The only thing I need from you, Brindle, is for you to step around to the other side of me," the rock said mysteriously.

"Oh!" Brindle said in surprise. "All right, then that is what I will do."

Brindle stepped around the other side of the rock, on the side with the field of flowers and she was blasted with the feelings of happiness, coming from all around her, and even coming now from her.

Sitting in the field of flowers were almost all of the friends that she had recently met and shared adventures with...

There was Brup... and his frog brother and sister, Brap and Brop... Cal the caterpillar now turned butterfly... Mari the horse... Benni the beaver... Elli the eagle... Leon the lion... Berri the bear... Sadie the Spider... Fanny the fairy... Toby the troll... the colored unicorns... Red, Blue, Yellow, Green, Purple, and Orange...

Even her monster friends were here... the Zesty Zombie... Savvy Skeleton... Ridiculous Rat... Grinning Ghost... Misunderstood

Medusa... Devilish Dragon... and the Sun shined down on top of them all.

There were colors and streamers everywhere, with tables and tables of food and drink of every kind. There was even a big cake with a single candle on top. And the cake had her name on it... it said, Brindle!

"What is all of this?" Brindle said, a little overwhelmed.

"It is your birthday, Brindle!" the Sun said from the sky.

"It is?" Brindle asked. "I didn't know that!"

"It is," the sun said. "I was there, bright and shining in the sky the day that you were born."

"Oh, my!" said Brindle. "Then this is all for me?"

"It is!" all of her friends cried out. "We wanted to show you just how much we love you and are glad to be your friends! You have taught us and helped us so much. We just wanted to show you how special you really are!"

Brindle had never felt so special or happy in her whole life as she went and joined her friends for her party adventure.

Afterward

Thank you for making it through to the end of *The Magic Unicorn*, let's hope it was enjoyable and fun reading that you can share again and again. Brindle the Magic Unicorn will always be here waiting for you to come back and share in her adventures.

Finally, if you really enjoyed this book, a review on Amazon is always appreciated!

Made in the USA
Middletown, DE
03 January 2021